# Range
# Boss

Center Point
Large Print

Also by D. B. Newton and available from
Center Point Large Print:

*Fury at Three Forks*
*Broken Spur*
*Syndicate Gun*
*Bullets on the Wind*
*Bounty on Bannister*

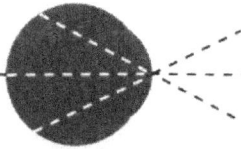

# Range Boss

# D. B. Newton

CENTER POINT LARGE PRINT
THORNDIKE, MAINE

This Center Point Large Print edition
is published in the year 2022 by arrangement with
Golden West Inc.

Originally published in the US by Pocket Books.

The text of this Large Print edition is unabridged.
In other aspects, this book may vary
from the original edition.
Printed in the United States of America
on permanent paper sourced using
environmentally responsible foresting methods.
Set in 16-point Times New Roman type.

ISBN 978-1-63808-529-4 (hardcover)
ISBN 978-1-63808-533-1 (paperback)


The Library of Congress has cataloged this record
under Library of Congress Control Number: 2022942410

# Range Boss

# CHAPTER I

It must have been someone's crude sense of humor that put the Willow Crossing cemetery on the trail leading into town; not just alongside it—say, on a prominent rise of land that would thereby earn the inevitable title of "Boothill"—but instead actually athwart the rutted wagontracks. So it was that the lone horseman, now lifting a slow haze of dust along that tawny road, found himself suddenly surrounded by an eerie, silent spread of sunken graves and rotted wooden headboards.

On either hand they stretched about him; and they were not few, because Willow Crossing, in the old cattle trail days, had enjoyed a pretty woolly reputation. But of course the old days had long since ended, as better rail facilities reduced the town's importance as a shipping point. No more was Willow Crossing in the headlines, or violent death a normal symbol of her days. As a result, the cemetery had long ago ceased its extraordinary growth.

Not many of the mounds or markers looked at all new; an oppressive sense of time past—of wasted lives, and of a lurid history best forgotten—hung heavily in the heated air above that desolate place. The rider on the bay gelding reined in—a tall man, well built, with a spare hardness in his rather lean frame. There was strength in the line of the jaw, in the solid set of the mouth that nevertheless had a quirk of humor at its corners. But the mouth was not smiling now, the smoke-gray eyes held a solemn frown.

For a long time he sat motionless, gazing about at the silent graves; then he swung down slowly, led his horse on trailing reins as he went among the scattered rows, searching. From the fact that he did not at once find what he was looking for, it was apparent the man was a stranger here. He seemed rather surprised when at last, his efforts actually met with success.

In an obscure corner of the lot a neglected, weed-grown mound had a weathered board at its head, set at a crazy angle, which bore the name "Les Thompson," and nothing more.

Halting in front of this board, the stranger looked at it with eyes that told nothing. He put up a lean hand, presently: jerked off an old stetson that was stained with sweat around the band, and stood like that in the hot blast of the sun—brown head bare, a tall figure in Levi's and Justin boots and a shirt that was sweatsoaked and streaked with alkali. Then he dragged the hat back on, and led his bronc again to the road and again mounted.

A very few minutes later, he came in on the town itself.

He found a straggle of buildings along either

side of the road, that here narrowly skirted the broad, shallow banks of a winding creek. The town was located at a point where the twin ribbons of the railroad, coming in from the northeast, crossed the creek on a high trestle; loading chutes stood along the bottoms, on a switch. The willows that gave the place its name hung motionless and drooping above the sunbright waters, and beyond the creek the rails were molten streaks of light across tawny sage flats before they disappeared in the haze of distance.

The stranger's bronc, coming in from the southward trail, took a narrow wagon bridge over the creek and stepped high and dainty as it crossed the shining tracks. They passed a weathered depot and freight shed, and so came into the main street that had once been the most hell-roaring strip north and west of the Pecos.

Today, in summer heat, this was a dusty, sleepy, forgotten village, living in gaudy dreams of its past. The stranger noticed empty buildings, their windows without glass and boarded up, or staring out upon the day like sightless eyes. From its unhealthy zenith as a cattleman's metropolis, Willow Crossing had shrunk to fit at last a more modest role—that of the average, prosperous cowtown, serving its own immediate range. The great railhead days of the big cattle drives were gone, for good.

He spotted the big hotel, half of its rooms

undoubtedly never used now. He marked its location; for his business lay there. But being thirsty and travelworn he put his mount first of all to the gnawed hitchpole fronting one of the two or three saloons that still operated, and swung down into ankledeep dust.

Water in a trough was handy and the bay gelding greeted this with pleasure, dipping its dust-caked muzzle into it eagerly and taking in the cool moisture with dainty sips. The man grinned, gave the sweaty neck an affectionate slap and then stepped up onto the wooden sidewalk and shoved through swinging doors, to the dim coolness of the saloon.

Like the hotel, this place looked too big for the trade it must do in these later days. Half of the long bar was apparently unused, and at the rear of the big room was a raised platform with battered footlights and a curtain hanging, rotten and moth-eaten. It must have been years since those curtains had closed on the last show, presented there in a time when the Lady Luck was a crowded, riotous place and money flowed freely across the whole length of the hardwood bar.

Now, as the stranger entered, he found the barnlike room gloomy and deserted except for a disconsolate-looking bartender, and a single customer lounging with one elbow on the mahogany and a half-filled glass before him. A pegleg tapped the floor when the barkeep moved over to greet the newcomer, sourly.

He ordered a drink, watched it poured and rang a coin across in payment. The apron pegged off toward a cash box. The stranger leaned there tiredly, letting the burn of the liquor into his throat slowly, glad of the cool silence, glad to ease muscles strained by hours of riding. The other drinker at the bar shifted for a look at the stranger, and the latter threw back an indifferent glance and suddenly a light hardened in the smoky grayness of his eyes.

A town marshal's badge made a tarnished gleam against the other's unbuttoned vest. Only by this would the newcomer have recognized him, although the face above it was at second look, a sort of flabby, coarsened caricature of one that had been familiar to him in the past, from photographs and the pen-and-ink drawing illustrating a magazine article, fifteen years ago.

To look at Vince Kirby now, he thought, you would hardly suppose that this was the town tamer whose fabulous gunswift and nerve had made legend, during the trail herd days at Willow Crossing.

Kirby paired the stranger's appraising glance, and interest flickered in the man's narrow eyes. He emptied his glass and edged casually along the bar, toward the newcomer.

"Just get in town?" he grunted.

The new man nodded.

He was thinking that Vince Kirby became less impressive, the nearer you saw him. What had been, in the old photographs, a face clean-chiseled and sharp, seemed blurred now and aged more than the lapsed time should have warranted. The eyes had pouches below them, and in the nose and cheeks there showed a fine network of ruptured, tiny veins, that only drink could have put there.

The eyes, however, were cold sober and there was a hint of suspicion in them. Vince Kirby said: "You look familiar to me. I'm wondering if I haven't seen you before?"

"I don't think so, Vince Kirby."

"But you know my name?"

"By reputation. I guess everybody has heard about you, and the old days."

The marshal only grunted; but visibly he was more than a little pleased. He seemed to expand a little, and turning he signaled the barkeep. "Let's have a drink on that, friend," he suggested.

For just a fraction of a second the stranger hesitated; then he shrugged. "Why not?"

The aproned tender filled the glasses. Lifting his, Vince Kirby said: "And your name, partner?"

"Thompson. Rick Thompson."

It meant nothing to the marshal, obviously. He threw off his drink quickly, set the glass down and watched the other as he drained his more

12

slowly. Then, because it was expected, the man named Thompson called for another round; but two drinks was his limit and so he left the third glass half filled, on the sticky surface of the bar.

Vince Kirby, he saw, was giving him a veiled scrutiny, that took in the trailstained length of him nor failed to note the filled shellbelt, the holster and polished gunbutt at the stranger's hip. Kirby himself wore crossed belts and two silver-mounted weapons—guns that were part of the old legend.

"You staying in Willow Crossing?" asked the marshal.

Plainly, the man's curiosity was roused—plagued by some vague memory that irritated him by its evasiveness. The stranger gave him no satisfaction. He said only: "Maybe—maybe not. I got some business to tend to, before I decide."

And after a few more words—formal and noncommital—he paid for his round of drinks and, dragging his stetson on more firmly, went out of the saloon. It seemed to him he could feel the marshal's narrow stare against his shoulders, speculatively, until the swinging batwings came to behind him and the hot blast of the sun was on him again.

Vague disappointment rode him as he went away from that chance meeting.

Not that the marshal and his legends had ever been an object of hero-worship for Rick

Thompson; on the contrary, there were personal reasons why he might have hated the very thought and name of Vince Kirby. But as a matter of fact, any such feelings had had plenty of time to bury themselves in the years since the killing of his brother Les.

He did not know now why the sight of Vince Kirby should put, instead, this unnamed regret inside him. It was regret, perhaps, at seeing a great man outlive his usefulness and come toward old age undistinguished and bearing few traces of what he had once been. . . .

Rick Thompson shrugged these idle thoughts aside, and went to the hitching pole to get his horse. They had come a long, hard trail and the bay could use a good feed of oats and a rubdown. But Rick decided to wait until after he had taken care of his business at the hotel. Best to know, first of all, whether he would be staying in town tonight or not.

He swung up to saddle, and headed his bronc toward the big, square bulk of the building he had spotted earlier. The hotel had a gallery across the front, a deep veranda with split reed rockers ranged along the rail. They were all empty. There was that dead feeling of any cowtown, on a hot summer day in the middle of the week.

Stepping down he snubbed the bay to a second hitchrack and moved up the broad, deepworn steps to the veranda. The wide door stood open;

he went through into a cool lobby, with desk and pigeonholed rack at the back under the stairs.

Here were sagging, overstuffed chairs and a sofa near the window, a worn carpet on the floor. A thin, pinkscalped man was sorting a handful of mail behind the desk. In a chair another man sat reading a newspaper; he held it before him in such a way that Rick Thompson could see only a steeple-topped hat above the paper, and crossed legs and feet encased in spurred boots that looked run down at the heels.

Thompson went straight to the desk. He told the hotelman: "I'm looking for M. J. Carlon—"

Whatever effect he expected from this statement, the one he got was startling. For a moment the man behind the desk could only stare at him, wordless; and from behind Rick came a rattle of the newspaper and seeing the hotelkeeper's scared eyes slide past him he turned quickly, took a look over his shoulder. The man in the overstuffed chair by the window raised quickly the paper he had lowered, ducked his head into it; Rick had only a glimpse of a dark face, a mustache and cruel, sharp eyes.

Irritation pricked him, his temper worn thin by tiredness. Turning back to the hotelman he said, flatly: "Well, what about it? I've got a letter in my pocket, from this Carlon hombre. He says to ask for him here at the desk of the hotel. Thompson is the name—"

15

Suddenly the other was stammering in reply, nervousness in him. "Yes, yes! Of course!" He kept looking past at the man across the lobby, and Rick got the definite feeling that he was scared and trying to warn him to greater secrecy.

"Room 16," the man was saying, in a voice that sounded hoarse with strain. "I'll take you up myself—"

"That ain't necessary," grunted Rick, starting to turn toward the stairs.

"Oh, but it is!" The hotelman was already tilting the dropleaf in the counter, sidling out and past Rick. Irritated, Thompson stood aside and then went after him, striding deliberately up the creaking stairs behind the little man's hurrying shape.

Something about this whole setup struck him, suddenly, as very queer. The deal that he and Carlon had discussed by mail had seemed like such an extraordinary bargain that he had suspected all along there must be a catch buried in it somewhere; now, after all those weary miles of riding, it looked as though he were going to learn just exactly where the joker lay.

He might have known real alarm, could he have seen the man in the lobby throw down his paper the moment Thompson had disappeared, and go hurrying out of the hotel with sudden, grim purpose in his movements. . . .

# CHAPTER II

The corridor on the hotel's second floor showed all the shabbiness of neglect and time. The carpet was quite worn through before each closed door, so that the bare boards showed, and in places gaudy, faded wallpaper hung in tatters. One wing of the building was still in regular use, however, and some efforts had been made to keep it in condition.

With Thompson following him the man headed straight for a door at the end of that wing. The stranger's long legs quickly distanced him, and coming abreast of the other Rick Thompson said sharply: "Who was that hombre down there in the lobby? The one you didn't like hearing what we said?"

"Why, what made you think—?" the other began, changed his tune when he saw Thompson's look. He shrugged, then. "That was Hank Brush. He's a Keystone rider—"

"Keystone?" The tall man frowned more darkly. That was the name of the ranch he had come all this way to purchase—honestly, he had hoped.

The man would answer no further questions. At the door of the end room—Number 16, by the numerals painted on the panel—he halted and rapped softly, in a manner that seemed meant for a signal. Afterwards there was silence for a

17

moment. Thompson plainly heard the creaking of the floor on the other side of the door, but no answer to the knock.

The hotelman said softly: "It's all right. This is Sam Hughes. There's a big, Texas-talking stranger out here asking for M. J. Carlon. Says his name is Thompson—"

At once a key clicked, and the door was thrown wide. The tall man found himself staring into a pair of brown eyes, set beneath brown curls and a wide brow in a face that was naturally tanned but seemed pale now under the weight of some strain.

The girl was tall, and she was well proportioned; the riding dress she wore just revealed the soft contours of her body. Her nose was rather short, her red lips full, her chin firm and a little stubborn. She was very young—not more than twenty-one, if that, Rick Thompson thought.

She said, on a half-breathless tone: "You are—?"

"I'm the man that's been corresponding with this Carlon hombre."

He reached into a pocket, brought out an envelope that was soiled by much handling. She seemed to recognize it.

"Come in," she said swiftly. And to the hotelman: "Thanks, Sam—a lot!"

"Sure," he answered.

He was about to turn away when he paused

to add, nervously: "That fellow Brush has been down in the lobby all afternoon. You suppose your uncle has guessed anything?"

Rick Thompson saw that news hit her, saw the alarm that built quickly into her eyes. She said only: "I—I hope not, Sam!"

Then the man was gone, and Rick had stepped into the hotel room and she had closed the door and put her back to it.

A quick glance over the room with its meagre furnishings showed that there was no one else here. Thompson turned to the girl, then, and in spite of himself there was suspicion and a little hardness in his tone. "Well," he demanded. "Where is he?"

"I am Mary Jane Carlon," she answered, simply.

It still took a minute for him to understand. When he did he frowned. "You wrote this letter? You put the ad in that Texas paper, offering the Keystone iron here at Willow Crossing for sale?"

"Yes, I did. I've been waiting for you to come. If you have the money with you—"

She faltered, at something she read in his look.

"Now, hold on just a minute!" Thompson's big-brimmed hat was off and he was turning it a little nervously in his rope-scarred hands, as he frowned at the girl. He didn't quite know how to tell her what he was thinking; the nice brown eyes, looking at him so levelly, made it hard to put his suspicions into words.

He steeled himself against them. "Look," he muttered, shortly. "I'm sure you won't mind my saying it, but seems to me there's something pretty doggone queer about this whole setup. You sure it's all open and above board?"

She did not take offense, as he had half expected she would; she seemed frightened, rather, and one brown hand came up to her throat as she stared at him. A pink tip of tongue came out and touched her lips. "Why—of course. Keystone is my ranch—it was left to me by my mother and dad, three years ago."

"What about this uncle I heard you mention?"

"Oliver Pierce. He's my guardian."

The man's frown deepened. "If you got a guardian then you aren't of age. What you trying to do—go over his head?"

"I *am* of age," she protested, quickly. "Nearly three months, now. But—" She made a despairing gesture. "Oh, it's very complicated. Won't you sit down, please, Mr. Thompson. And let me try to explain?"

He looked around. There was one rickety rocking chair near the window, and the bed. No place else to sit. He took the chair, hearing it creak as he let himself into it stiffly. The girl had left her post at the door now, but she seemed too wrought-up to sit anywhere. She began pacing up and down instead, between the bed and the window. Finally she stopped that and faced

Rick Thompson with a determined gesture.

"I do own the Carlon ranch," she began, earnestly. "It's a good spread—just as I told you in my letters. Good grass, a section of alfalfa for winter feeding; and the winters are mild in this valley. Our beef stock is the best, though it hasn't been very well tended for the past three years."

"Yes, it sounds good," he admitted, coldly. "Too good, for the price you're asking. Too darn much of a bargain."

"It is a bargain. And I wouldn't sell, except I—I just don't know anything else to do! I was born on the Keystone, Mr. Thompson. My folks are buried there. I love every acre of it, but—" She shook her head, and her brown eyes had a hint of tears in them. "My uncle—I'm helpless against him!

"Oliver Pierce has been my guardian; was appointed to manage Keystone for me, after the accident that took my parents. He's run things to please himself. He has his own men working there—Brag Nabor is foreman, and the rest are about the same stripe. Toughs, and gunfighters! They've sold off most of the stock, let the rest run wild in the breaks. Since I came of age, I've been practically a prisoner. Sometimes I—I even think my uncle would have me killed, if he could think of a sure way to do it and take over the property, to add to what he already holds!"

Thompson was out of his chair, with a quick,

easy movement, his face dark. "Good Lord!" he exclaimed. "If that's the truth, why can't you do something about it? Put the law on him! You got a right to have him kicked plumb off the place, if it really belongs to you now—"

The look she gave him was full of lost helplessness. He knew a sudden uneasy questioning. It was a wild sounding story she was telling him, and a little hard to believe. And yet, despite her manner, he hated to think that this pretty girl might have something wrong inside her head, making her entertain false, half-crazy notions of persecution. He'd known a man like that once. It had been a most uncanny experience. . . .

She said: "It's not as simple as it sounds. My uncle is the big man in this town and range. He owns the Pierce Land and Cattle Company, and influence enough to make anyone hesitate to cross him. As for the law—well, hereabouts that's Vince Kirby, and Kirby is my uncle's special friend. It's a long way to the county seat and sheriff's office, and nobody there pays much attention to anything that happens at Willow Crossing."

"I see."

Mary Jane Carlon made a helpless gesture. "I didn't know any other way. I had to get free of Oliver Pierce—I was afraid for my very life. I managed to insert an ad in the papers, without his knowledge. Sam Hughes, the hotelman,

22

helped me; so did old Nat Fenwick, the cook at Keystone. When your letters came, they sneaked them in to me and took back my answers and mailed them. And then, when you wrote that you were coming to look over the proposition, I managed to sneak out despite the guard my uncle kept over me, and get here to the hotel. Since then Sam has been hiding me in this room, while Keystone riders combed the hills hunting for me. . . ."

It was indeed an improbable tale—the wildest Rick Thompson had ever heard. But something made him hear her out, soberly. Frowning, he said: "And that was one of your uncle's riders down in the lobby? When he heard me ask for 'M. J. Carlon' then, he realized you were here. Now he's gone to report to your uncle."

"I—hadn't thought of that!" She had stopped her pacing, gone quickly pale with fear. She blurted: "You—you'd better leave."

He answered harshly: "A little late, isn't it, to start worrying about dragging a stranger into trouble? Just what was your idea—I'd buy Keystone from you, and along with it all your trouble with Pierce? But I guess that was all right with you, just so long as you got your money and got out from under, yourself—"

Thompson started to turn away, angrily, but her hand caught his sleeve pleadingly. "I—I know it wasn't fair!" she cried. "I've been so desperate

I didn't think it through. But at least I've been frank with you, Mr. Thompson! I've told you the whole situation; and what's more I've offered you Keystone at a price that's little more than a fraction of what it's worth. You see—you're a man; you can fight! And I—I rather thought a bargain like this one would be worth fighting for!"

There was truth in what she said. It made him turn back more slowly, to look down into her brown eyes. She looked hurt, and lonely—and lovely.

"Forgive me," he muttered suddenly. "You're right of course. It would take a man of pretty mean spirit not to realize that, even with all the strings attached, this is a proposition worth buying into. Nothin's worth having that don't take a scrap to get, and hold! But—"

He shrugged, then. "I'm not in a position to fight. I'm sorry, but that's how it is. My hands are tied."

"Of course." Her voice was slow, leaden. "It hadn't occurred to me that you might have a—a wife, and family, to consider—"

"Not that." Somehow Rick Thompson found himself coloring a little. "No, it's not anything like that holding me back. The fact is, this money I had intended investing in your ranch isn't my own, and so I can't afford to risk it recklessly.

"It's the life savings of three old cowpunchers—

stove-up old relics who put their money together and commissioned me to find a place where they could retire and spend their last years on their own land. The 'Mossyhorn Pool,' they call themselves for a joke. In return for handling the investment for them I'm to have the foreman's job; probably, some day, the ranch itself."

He shook his head. "So I guess you can see my responsibility. Even if it is a bargain, I have no right to risk this money and drag those three old men into a fight that's not their own. That's what I meant when I said my hands were tied."

"I see—" The girl's pretty face clouded, and she moved blindly away from him to the window where sunlight made a hot bright square upon her. "That—makes it entirely different, of course—"

She stopped. Rick saw her back stiffen, as her glance caught something in the street below the window. Quickly he moved up, looked past her brown head and saw it too.

Hank Brush was coming back toward the hotel at a quick, nervous stride that kicked up puffs of yellow dust from the still street's surface. There were two others with him; Thompson recognized the flabby shape of the town marshal, and saw another solid, chunky figure in a gray suit, pantlegs tucked into Justin half boots, a gray stetson set squarely. He could not make out the features of this third one, but the solid stride of the man gave a sense of power and self importance.

He said quickly; "That's Oliver Pierce?"

"Yes."

She whirled about. Thompson had moved so close behind her, to look past her through the window, that her upturned face was only inches from his own as she turned and her soft hair touched his cheek. She had a clean, healthy outdoor smell about her. Then he stepped back a pace in some confusion, and she was saying breathlessly:

"They're coming up here! You—you'd better hurry. There's a back stairs you can use to avoid any risk of a run-in with them!"

His dark face hardened. "And what happens to you?"

The stiffness ran out of her; her shoulders slumped, and though she tried to smile there was a dead defeat mirrored in her pretty face. "I'll be all right," she said, tonelessly.

But Rick Thompson read the fear in her— the utter terror of that man coming toward the hotel now with Brush and the marshal flanking him.

He took one more look into the street, saw the three of them halted down there talking. Vince Kirby turned on his heel suddenly, walked away. Pierce and his gunman came on up the broad steps to the veranda. Apparently, the girl's uncle thought he could handle this situation without resort to the lawman.

Then Thompson guessed differently. It occurred to him suddenly that Vince Kirby must have been sent around in order to cover that same rear entrance Mary Jane Carlon had urged him to take—

Quickly, he moved to the door, unlocked it, looked out into the deserted hall. Sound carried clearly up the stairwell, through the thin walls of the rickety old building. At that moment heavy boots came tramping into the lobby below and a booming voice sounded: "Where is she?"

"I—I don't know what you mean, Mr. Pierce," came the frightened voice of the little hotelman. The words were broken off by a sharp splat, as of a fist connecting, and then something hit the floor with a jarring thud.

"Don't lie to me!" thundered Oliver Pierce.

A third speaker—the gunman, Hank Brush— muttered something. Something about "Room 16."

"Let's go then," answered Pierce. He added: "I'll settle with you later, Sam Hughes—"

"By God!" the scared hotelman shrieked across the quiet. "If you hurt her, Ollie Pierce! If you so much as—"

The voice trailed off uselessly, as two sets of boots began to shake the treads of the rickety stairway. Rick Thompson closed the door, stood there a moment with one hand on the knob and the other moving to finger the butt of his holstered sixgun.

He knew, suddenly, that everything this girl had told him was the truth; that she stood very much in danger from that pair coming up the creaking stairs. That no element of the story she had told him, however fantastic it had sounded, but was based in sober fact.

And he knew, with quick resolution, that there was only one course he could follow.

# CHAPTER III

He whirled toward her. "You have a paper and pencil?"

"No, I—" She was staring at him, at something she read in his grim expression but failed to understand.

"Here!" he muttered. "This will do."

From a pocket he had taken the soiled envelope containing Mary Jane Carlon's letter. He slipped out the paper, turned it over, and leaning it against the closed door wrote on the blank side hurriedly with a chewed stub of pencil:

"For one dollar and other considerations I do hereby sell to Rickart Thompson half interest in Keystone Ranch, and in all lands, stock, and buildings appertaining."

"Sign right here," he said crisply, motioning her to him. "I don't know whether this is legal or not, but it sounds good enough to me."

The girl hung back, hesitating. He snapped his fingers in impatience.

"We haven't got much time," he prodded her. "They're right outside the door!"

She moved forward then, and without a word took the pencil stub and wrote her name with a firm, strong hand, while he held the paper against the door for her.

As she finished he folded the paper, tucked it into his shirt pocket behind his Bull Durham sack. He barely had time to drag a bulging leather wallet, cracked and sweatstained, from his hip pocket and thrust it into the girl's hands, when heavy fingers fell upon the knob of the door and without any ado it was shoved fiercely open.

The gray-clothed, gray-hatted man who filled the doorway, Hank Brush behind him, was stocky and powerfully built. He had florid features, a reddish tinge in the crisp, kinky hair that showed under the edge of the hat, at his temples. Rick Thompson judged his age at about forty-five.

Oliver Pierce ran a quick, restless glance over Thompson's face, over the furnishings of the shabby little room, and then let it rest on his niece's wide-eyed, frightened face. He was the first to speak.

"So!" he grunted. "This is where you've been, all the time. All the time I've had our men combing the range for you, worried to death over thoughts of what might have happened."

Mary Jane's eyes flashed with anger. "I can just bet you've been worried!" she bit at him.

Danger flickered in his own tawny eyes. He swung them on Rick Thompson. "Just where do *you* fit into this, Mister?" Nastiness twisted his thick lips into a smirk. "Did you sign the register 'Mister and Missus—'?"

Thompson's left fist arced, sharply, and

smashed the words against the big man's lips with a blow that took Oliver Pierce completely by surprise, sent him slamming back against the door jamb and into Hank Brush who yelled and moved out of the way.

Pierce caught himself. Hot color had poured upward into his face and he hunched his shoulders as though he would start forward, but Thompson's right hand rested on the holstered gun and that stopped him.

"If you can't talk anything but dirt," he said, bleakly, "maybe you better get out!"

Oliver Pierce put up a hairy fist, wiped it across his bruised lips and glanced at his knuckles as though looking for blood. He lifted his hard stare at Thompson. "You're not going to be glad you did that!" he muttered.

The stranger returned his glance without speaking. And even with Hank Brush backing him, Pierce did not seem to want to buck that gun which was already under Thompson's hand, though still holstered. He shrugged, turned again to the girl.

"Are you ready to cut out this foolishness and be starting back for the ranch?" he demanded coldly. "I hope you realize what this little three day escapade has cost, in the wages of the men who had to be taken off of other work in order to go looking for you. I hope you've got a good story thought up to excuse yourself."

She retorted, with spirit: "You know I'm no longer answerable to you, not since my last birthday! If I ran away from the ranch, it was for a very good reason—to escape the imprisonment in which you've held me, and the death you'd deal out for me if you thought you could get away with it!"

Her words lashed out upon a sudden silence. They washed all expression from the face of Oliver Pierce, and the big man turned and exchanged an empty glance with Hank Brush.

"I swear, it's unbelievable!" he murmured. "If there were only witnesses to report that kind of talk to a judge, he'd be very apt to doubt Miss Carlon's mental fitness and appoint me her permanent guardian."

"Cut out the acting!" Rick Thompson spoke sharply, cutting across the girl's exclamation of horror. "You know there's nothing wrong with her mind—or with her ability to see through you and your cheap ambitions, either. And now I'll tell you something you don't know:

"You're through running Keystone. You're all washed up out there!"

The big man's eyes got narrow and mean. "Who says so?"

"I do." Thompson brought out the bill of sale, unfolded it for Pierce to see the writing. "I'm Miss Carlon's partner, as of right now. I have just bought half interest in the spread—and I'm telling you that if you venture to set foot on either half, I'm gonna personally throw you off."

Oliver Pierce read the bill of sale at a glance. His mouth twisted. He shot a look at the girl.

"Why, you fool!" he snapped. "What have you let this stranger put over on you, when I wasn't here to protect your interests? Just how much do you know about this—partner—of yours?"

"That wallet she's holding is full of money—good, U. S. dollars," Rick Thompson cut back at him. "And she knows about me that I won't let you put over any fast ones. This thing is on a different basis now—and instead of a girl you've got a man and a gun against you. That's the main thing she needs in a partner."

He jerked his head toward the open door. "Now, let's see the pair of you drag yourselves out of here, and leave Miss Carlon alone. . . ."

They went, but not before Oliver Pierce had measured Thompson with his cold stare, and told him in a flat voice weighted with threat: "You're a very foolish young man!" Then Rick was scowling at the closed door, all that had been said going through his mind.

He hardly was aware of Mary Jane's hand placed upon his arm, until her voice came to him, tight with emotion.

"I'm afraid!"

He turned to her, smiled a little bleakly. "No need of that. Pierce's hands are tied now, and

33

there's little danger of his trying to harm you."

"But you don't understand! It's not myself I'm worried about. I'm thinking of you—and of those three old cowpunchers. I've gone and dragged you all into this mess, and I'm ashamed—"

Rick Thompson shook his head. He was very close to her, looking at her wide brown eyes and her very red lips, slightly parted now. He told her soberly:

"You didn't drag anybody into anything. I bought into this fight on my own accord—and because I know old Montana and Andy and Bill would have wanted me to!

"Sure we've got a fight on our hands now, but it's just the kind of fight those three old hellions would itch to tackle!"

"But—" She dropped her glance before his own intent gaze, and she indicated the cracked leather wallet in her hands. "This money . . . The bargain was for the whole ranch, not for a mere half interest!"

He said: "It's still a bargain! If Keystone is half the spread you say it is, we'd be robbing you at the other price. Let's forget the details, shall we, until after the boys arrive and we've had a chance to look the situation over? As I see it, we're all in this thing together, and that's far enough ahead to figure. Agreed?"

She smiled, suddenly—a frank, friendly grin that put little wrinkles at the base of her nose and touched Rick warmly. A strong, brown hand was thrust at him. "It's agreed!" she exclaimed, and they shook hands.

"Get ready to ride," he said then. "Do you have a bronc here in town?"

"No. Nat Fenwick, the ranch cook, sneaked me into town under a tarp in the back of his wagon."

"I'll rent one for you then, at the livery. I have a telegram to send, too. Look for me in about fifteen minutes, and we'll head for Keystone."

She said, "All right." And added: "Be careful, won't you?"

"Of course."

There was no one in the dingy hall, no one on the stairs. In the lobby below Rick found the hotelman, Sam Hughes, behind his desk, and the little man's jaw was swollen and a livid bruise was forming there. He was trembling as he nodded to Rick, and the latter went over and said bluntly:

"Will Oliver Pierce make trouble for you now?"

"I imagine he will," the little man was plainly frightened, and unnerved by the blow. "He's plenty mad at me for helping Miss Carlon. And he's a tough kind of enemy."

"Keep a gun handy," Rick Thompson suggested. "And don't take anything off the hombre. If he gets too much for you, maybe we at Keystone can give you some help."

Sam Hughes stared at him. "You're dealing

yourself into this? You're going to buck Ollie Pierce, yourself?"

"That's right," answered Thompson, and walked out of the dark building.

The street was hot, and still, and soundless. Thompson's bay gelding, at the tie rack, swished its tail at the flies. No other life stirred, though he stood in the shadow by the door and watched for a long moment before he crossed the veranda, went down the wide warped steps and moved around the hitchrack toward the bronc.

Somehow, he had rather expected Oliver Pierce to meet him with further trouble; but there were no signs of it. So Thompson found stirrup and swung astride, and headed down the wide, dusty street toward the shining lines of the railway, and the old depot and freight shed and loading pens.

The rattle of a telegraph key sounded in the stillness as he neared. He left the bay in the shade and rang his spurs across the splintered depot platform to the agent's open window. A reedy, baldheaded man was shutting off the key, removing headphones, as Thompson's shadow fell across the sill.

"I'd like to send a wire."

The man shoved over a pencil and pad of blanks. Thompson already had the message worked out in his mind and he wrote quickly.

He passed the pad back through the window

and waited while the operator read over the message, counted the words, and gave him the price. He paid with loose change from his pocket.

Turning, then, he was more than a little startled to see Vince Kirby leaning thick shoulders against the depot's warped clapboards, not ten feet away.

Rick Thompson halted, returning the marshal's slow stare. He didn't know how Kirby could have moved that close without his hearing, because the old planks of the wooden platform rested on rotted stringers and gave easily to the weight of a footstep. Anyhow, there he stood and it was obvious to Rick that Pierce had sent him.

Now Kirby eased erect and unfolded his arms, letting them dangle at his sides. The badge on his unbuttoned vest gleamed dully, and so did the silver work on the twin guns strapped to his thighs. His eyes were sharp but his voice casual as he said, "Finished your business here?"

"Yeah, I guess so."

"Good." An amused look crossed the other's glance, as though he were secretly laughing at a joke of his own. "You can come along with me, then."

"Where to?"

"The jail."

Thompson looked at him blankly, beginning to feel a crawling of anger. "Are you arresting me?"

"There's a town statute against carrying guns within the city limits. It was passed back in the trail town days, and it was never revoked. You're busting it now."

A scowl darkened the stranger's face. "This is a damn poor joke, Kirby. Something Ollie Pierce suggested, I suppose." He added, impulsively, "How come you didn't try to enforce this spavined law of yours when we were drinking together in the saloon, a while ago? I was packing my iron then, you'll remember."

Vince Kirby shrugged. "You were acting peaceable then. I generally don't bother a gent until I see how his intentions are. Looks now like yours aren't so good; so I'm bringing the law to bear and locking you up.

"Come on! Peel off that belt and holster and drop your iron. I don't intend to take any foolishness from you!"

# CHAPTER IV

As he gave his order the gun-marshal's hand moved back and the fingers curled around the butt of one of those silver-mounted guns. He drew it half way out of the cutdown holster and waited that way to see what the other man was going to do.

For a long moment Rick Thompson hesitated; then he gave an angry shrug, and his own lean brown hands went to the buckle of his belt and jerked it loose. Seeing him comply with instructions, Vince Kirby smiled a little and let his half-drawn weapon plop back into its sheath.

"Throw it right here at my feet—" he ordered.

Just then the tongue of the belt swung free and Rick Thompson gave a quick flip of the wrist and let go. The heavy holster flew at Vince Kirby; he gave back a step, half startled. And immediately Rick Thompson was moving in on him.

He crowded the marshal back against the clapboards, both hands shooting forward and out. They struck Kirby's wrists as the man made a stabbing movement toward his guns, and knocked his hands away from the gunhandles.

With the same motion Thompson disarmed the lawman and when he stepped back, Kirby's own silverhandled sixguns were in the stranger's hands, and lined squarely on the gunman's soft belly.

"Goddam—!" sputtered the marshal, and fell silent.

There was no witness except the baldheaded telegrapher, staring wide-eyed from his window a half dozen feet away. But this was an event that no one who knew Vince Kirby's old reputation would ever have thought possible—to see the famous gunslick cleaned of his own weapons and hauled up at the point of their muzzles.

He seemed incapable of believing it himself. He stood there, legs spread, hands working spasmodically above the lips of his empty holsters. And Rick Thompson returned his stare, cool and unruffled, and he said:

"I'm afraid you've slipped a little since the old trail drive days. Or maybe you never were quite the bigtime gunman your rep made you out to be. Because I can't imagine any one being taken in by a simple trick like that one!"

Kirby found his tongue. His chest was laboring under the hard control he put over his temper, and he said tightly:

"You'll live to regret this!"

Thompson made no answer. He glanced down, spotted his own belt and holster where they lay on the splintered platform not far away. He shoved one of the marshal's guns under his arm, reached with free hand and got his own weapon. And

40

then, one by one, Vince Kirby's famous silver-mounted pistols made streaks of hot sunlight as their captor tossed them up onto the red shingles of the depot roof.

"You can find you a ladder and get those back," Rick Thompson suggested. "I'll be out of town by then, so you won't have to worry about arresting me for the time being." He added: "Of course, I might be back any time!"

Vince Kirby seemed beyond words, but his narrow glance was eloquent of his hatred. And once more, Thompson got the feeling that this man had half-way recognized him—that the speculation he read in Kirby's look was a questioning, an effort to remember where he might have seen the stranger's face before, or someone who closely resembled him.

Rick Thompson could have enlightened him, but he did not bother. Instead, he buckled his gun and belt into place and then turned and placed one hard, rope-scarred hand upon the sill. "You'll send that wire out right away, Sparks?"

The telegrapher's head bobbed emphatically. "Yes! Yessiree!" He scurried to his key, a tremble of excitement in him.

"Thanks," said Thompson, and turning his back on Vince Kirby he went again to his horse and mounted up.

He did not look back as he rode away from the station, but he knew Kirby was standing where he had been left, staring after him with hatred in his eyes, the famous paired guns gleaming on the depot roof just out of his reach.

"He'll find it kind of hot, crawling around on those shingles after them," Rick thought, and couldn't help a smile.

Then he thought of more important things, and his smile sobered.

Mary Jane saw him from her hotel room window, as he came riding back up the street trailing a dappled gray livery bronc. He returned her signal, and as she disappeared hauled in and waited like that, sitting saddle while he rolled a smoke and kept a close eye on the stillness of the town.

He hoped the girl would waste no time. Oliver Pierce had had plenty of chance to start something with him, and had failed to show, but nevertheless Rick Thompson wanted to put this town behind him.

By this time, Vince Kirby might have his guns back and be in a mood to do something about that scene at the railroad depot. Thompson didn't want to have to face him now. Not with the safety of the girl dependent on him.

But now light footsteps sounded from the hotel veranda and Mary Jane came hurrying down the steps. She carried a small suitcase and Rick took this from her, and leaning from saddle gave her a hand up to the back of the livery bronc. Then he handed her the reins and quickly lashed the suitcase to his own saddle strings.

"You lead the way," he said quietly, "I'll follow up and keep an eye on our backs . . ."

However, no move was made to stop them. They went up the long street with its empty buildings staring sightless upon the afternoon, and there were few people on the sidewalks and no one who paid much attention as they rode out.

Rick Thompson decided that Oliver Pierce was convinced he could make no move against this pair within the town itself. But that didn't preclude a possibility of trouble, once they hit the open range; Hank Brush, for example, could have been sent ahead to stop them before reaching Keystone. Thinking this, Rick told the girl:

"Maybe you better take the long way."

She nodded, apparently understanding.

They had left the last buildings of town behind them now, and the road stretched ahead like a powdery white ribbon angling northward across the flats of sage and bluestem. Off to the right a red rim shimmered low against the sky. Buttes spotted the broken land ahead.

After a couple of miles Mary Jane left the road and put her bronc into a shallow draw that led off toward the rim, northeast. Rick followed, keeping his eye peeled for any sign of trouble. There was none—no sound other than the rattle of their horses' hoofs in the stony draw, no movement other than the high circling of a hawk on rising currents of heated air.

They came out of the draw, went up a shaley slope crowned with scrub growth. As they topped it Rick pulled in for a moment, looked back.

Far away through the clear, warm day showed the flashing streak of the railroad, the green of willows along the river, the huddled roofs and criss-crossed streets of the town. He saw a tawny road, looping southward across the dry plains. A thoughtful frown came into his eyes and stayed there as he put his bronc on after the girl's.

Now they rode over slightly rolling acres of sage and bunch grass, with small broadleafed cactus scattered through. The red rim hung at their right and they went parallel with it. The white sun marched overhead, and there was silence all around them. The lone hawk made a graceful sweeping curvet, its wings spread motionlessly; then it sailed off and disappeared somewhere behind the rim.

Rick Thompson pulled up even with the girl's mount. He was still frowning, and he said now, "Coming into town, I noticed the way they've got the graveyard laid out. Kind of gruesome."

"Isn't it?" she agreed. "That's from the old days. Someone thought it might be a good idea for trail hands larruping into town to get a good look at Boothill. Imagined it would quiet them down some."

44

"Did it do any good?"

She made a gesture. "A lot of men got planted there."

"Were you here in the old days—the wild days?" he asked, after a bit.

"Yes, for part of them. I was a little girl, of course. And my folks were careful I didn't see too much of the goings on. But they weren't always successful. I saw Vince Kirby kill a man one day, in front of the Lady Luck. It scared me into a crying fit."

"What was your impression of Vince Kirby when you were little?"

Mary Jane turned suddenly, gave Rick a level, thoughtful look. "All these questions," she said. "You're asking them for a purpose, aren't you?"

He nodded. "Yes. In a moment I'll tell you why."

"Well—" She took a deep breath, canted her head a little with a little pucker between her arched brows, as she looked at shimmering distance and also into the remembered past.

"It's very hard, knowing Kirby as he is today, to remember my early impressions of him. He seemed very tall, of course—straight and slim and striking. He wore his hair long, almost to his shoulders, and his clothes were fine and expensive. I used to see him prowling through the town on his beat, the sun flashing from the handles of his guns—how those guns used to frighten me! And everybody stepped out of his way, even the toughest Texas gunmen. But—"

She hesitated, and Rick waited with his eyes carefully on her pretty face.

"I know my father never had much use for Kirby, in spite of all the legends. He used to say that Kirby was no better than a killer himself, who happened to take the town council's pay for his shootings and pose as a champion of law and justice. And though Vince Kirby must have known about that talk, he never did anything to stop my dad from making it."

Rick Thompson's thoughts had turned inward, conjuring up the picture of Vince Kirby as the man must have looked in the days of the legend— and comparing it with the flabby, graying hulk of a man whom he had bested on the depot platform, hardly an hour ago. Time, he mused, is a strange thing—

He caught the girl's glance turned on him, the quizzical look of her brown eyes. Mary Jane said, "You were going to tell me your reasons—"

"Oh," he nodded slowly; his voice was without expression as he answered her. "It's just that— that Vince Kirby once killed my brother."

He saw her eyes widen, her lips part to shape words that she did not speak. He went on, in the same tone:

"I was only a kid myself, then. Les was some years older, and wild. He left home to join up

46

with a trail outfit, came to Willow Crossing—and we never saw him again. But it was in the papers, how Vince Kirby claimed to have caught him robbing an express office here and had to kill him."

"How—terrible!" cried Mary Jane. "You must have hated Kirby for that, all these years!"

"No," he said, quickly. "As I said, Les had always been pretty wild; and we knew Kirby's reputation as an honest lawman. It nearly broke my mother's heart, of course, but we never questioned the story Vince Kirby told.

"Today was the first time I'd ever ranged as far north as Willow Crossing. I've always had a sort of morbid interest in coming, though. Riding in, I hunted Les Thompson's grave in the Boothill, and found it—or what's left of it. But still, until I laid eyes on Kirby for the first time, for myself, it had never occurred to me to wonder about that old killing. To wonder if the whole story had been told, or if maybe my brother had really been as bad as was made out at the time."

He nodded slowly, answering the question in her eyes. "Yes. From what I know of Kirby now, I'm beginning to wonder if the man isn't a damn liar. And if all these years the name of Les Thompson hasn't born a stain it never deserved! Because if I thought that was true—"

His voice, rising in anger, dropped and left the sentence unfinished. For a moment there was only the *plop-plop* of their horses' hoofs on the hard earth, the creak of saddle leather.

Mary Jane said, slowly, "I remember that express office robbery. Or, rather, of course, I mean I remember hearing about it. I had forgotten the name of the man who was killed, but I do know there was always some mystery about it. You see—they never did find the money that was stolen."

Rick Thompson took that in silence. Whatever he was thinking then he left unsaid.

They came down the bank of a shallow, swift-running stream, waited for the broncs to drink before they pushed on across the pebbly bottom. Then, following the course of the rivulet, they dropped down through slanting hills and came at last in view of a wide, shallow basin.

It was good grazing land. This stream they followed, flowing down from the rim, kept those acres well watered and green. They skirted a small band of whitefaced cattle, and Rick Thompson saw the Keystone iron burnt on them. But there wasn't the amount of beef this graze should have supported.

Then, in a stand of cottonwood ahead, he sighted the white shimmer of a neatly painted ranch house, with bunkhouse and barn and other buildings beyond. Mary Jane Carlon pointed.

"There's Keystone," she said.

# CHAPTER V

As they cantered in on the spread, he saw that she was tense and her face showed pale beneath its tan. He told her quickly: "Now, just relax! There may be some bad moments ahead of us but we'll get through them, and we'll handle this tough crew. How many riders are there?"

"Nine, Brag Nabor is foreman. They'll follow his lead, whatever he decides to do. And he isn't going to like this!"

"Forget Nabor. These hardcase characters are mostly bluff. You have to bluff right back."

All she said was, "Wait 'til you see him . . ."

But the ranch headquarters seemed deserted as they neared. Silence hung over the place. A couple of horses running in the starveout was the only sign of life they caught at first. Rick Thompson grunted. "Looks like we beat them in. Maybe they're all out in the hills hunting for you."

"I see smoke coming from the cookshack," said Mary Jane. "And—there's Nat!"

She kicked the livery bronc forward and Thompson followed. The slight, stooped figure of a man coming from the cookshack doorway, pail in hand, turned sharply as he heard the drum of their hoofbeats nearing. The westering sun was in his eyes and he put up a shading hand to squint against it. Then he threw aside the pail and came hobbling, to take the girl's reins as she pulled up.

"Janie!" he cried, in a cracked and aging voice. Alarm was in his tone. "Why in the world did you come back here? Don't you know—?"

His jaw clamped shut and he went narrow-eyed and suspicious as he got his first good look at the stranger with her. Both Rick and the girl were out of saddle by then and Mary Jane made brief introductions, and told the old man as best she could, in a few words, the changes that had come in the Keystone setup.

Nat Fenwick gave Thompson another, closer look of shrewd appraisal, and as he took in the size of the newcomer and the competent look of the sixgun on his hard thigh, something of respect came into his glance.

"So you're buying in? And you think you can handle that crew of hellions? Well—mebbe you can make a showing, at that. If you can get around Brag Nabor!"

Rick knew at once that he and this tough little oldster would get along. He said: "What do you think we ought to do with Nabor and his crowd?"

"Fire 'em!" the other replied promptly. "Clean house here at Keystone—except for me, of course! I wrangled cows for the Carlons 'til rheumatism took me outa the saddle, and I've wrastled frypans for 'em ever since. Try gettin' rid of me now and you'll know you've tangled with somethin'!"

Rick smiled. "If three people can run a ranch the size of Keystone," he said, "it looks like we're the three that's going to try. Do you know how much time the crew has coming?"

"There'll be a paybook in the desk in the office," Mary Jane suggested.

"Get it, while I'm taking care of the horses. We'll clean the slate once and for all, first move we make."

Old Nat executed a warped kind of jig step. "Hot damn!" he crowed. "This, I been waiting for a long time! It's been bad enough, watching that pack of rats louse up the old Keystone, without having to wrastle grub for them all and get kicked around by that scrub bully, Nabor!"

He added: "Better look alive, though, 'cause they'll be trailing in for supper pronto. This past week, Pierce has had 'em looking for you, Janie. But today he pulled them off that job and started 'em chousing strays down out of them breaks below the rim wall. Understand they's a buyer due pretty quick."

When he had taken care of the horses, Rick Thompson went into the house. It was a big place, furnished with care and showing the loving attention of the two women who had lived there. In a dark and musty office off the hall he found Mary Jane Carlon standing, frowning at a big rolltop desk.

"It's locked," she told him.

Rick fetched a poker from the fireplace in the living room and using it as a crowbar snapped the lock and rolled the big top back. In one of the cluttered pigeonholes they found the paybook, with each Keystone rider credited with the wages he had coming.

Thompson said: "Pay them out of the money in the wallet. It'll cut into our cash supply, and leave us shorthanded for a crew; but as Nat says, the first thing is to get rid of that tough bunch of your uncle's.

"After supper," he added, scowling at the mess of papers in the desk, "we'll go through this stuff and try to find out just what shape the ranch is in. No telling what we'll find, after your uncle has been running it for three years to suit himself—"

Just then Nat Fenwick's voice called excitedly: "Riders coming!"

Turning quickly he strode through the quiet house and out to the deep veranda. Sunset was not far off; a golden glow spread over the rich green bottoms, made the far rim a crimson streak of fire along the horizon. Against this he saw the black dots of nearing riders, and heard the muffled thud of their broncs running across the grass.

As the three came nearer he turned to Mary Jane, behind him on the porch. "Brag Nabor?"

"Not one of those," she said, shaking her head. "He'll be forking a big, ewe-necked gray."

The trio came into the yard, and Rick Thompson saw at a glance they were all of a type—hardcase saddle toughs. No wonder, he thought, the girl had been afraid—alone on the ranch with nine such men, and no one but the old cook to look to for help.

As they reined in, swinging down, Rick Thompson came out of the porch shadows and called out crisply: "Don't unsaddle—except you in the middle, forking that Keystone bronc. Fetch your warsacks out of the bunkhouse, because you're drawing your time and leaving. Right now!"

Turning, they stared up at him, their faces showing savage disbelief. One cursed and said heavily: "What the hell!"

"Who are you, telling us what to do?" another demanded. And then Mary Jane Carlon stepped to the rail where they could see her. Quick astonishment was printed plainly on their faces.

"There's been a change," she told them quietly. "You aren't needed on Keystone anymore. If you'll come into the office I'll settle with each of you for what's due you."

A moment's hesitation; then the man who had spoken first gave a growl and said, "I reckon I'll wait until Brag shows up. Maybe so he'll have something he wants to say about this . . ."

They were all going to wait for Brag. Nevertheless, they didn't go so far as to unsaddle their horses. They let them stand on trailed reins and walked over to the bunkhouse.

Rick Thompson watched that door nervously, half expecting to have a bullet come at him out of the darkness. But presently the three straggled out again. One took a seat on a bench under the bunkhouse. The other pair slouched over to a cottonwood and settled down with their backs against the bole, and one took out a pocketknife, snapped open the blade, and began whittling as he whistled tonelessly between his teeth.

After ten minutes had passed, two more of the crew came in together. There were the same questions, the same challenging scowls as they heard what Rick Thompson had to say. One of this pair joined the others under the tree. The second took his bronc to a water trough, then climbed up to the top rail of the corral beside the barn and perched there, silently. Waiting, there was the same calm assurance in them all. Thompson, glancing from one to another, caught open, mocking sneers on their hard faces, as they measured him and waited with wolfish eagerness for Brag Nabor to come and put him in his place.

Time ran out. Rick felt the tension but would not let himself show it. The shadows grew longer;

the band of darkness slid up the big cottonwood until only its upper branches still twinkled in a flow of golden light.

Rick, tired of standing, eased down onto one of the veranda steps, carefully adjusted the hang of his holster and then set about rolling a smoke, for all the world as though he were merely passing a quiet lazy hour before the rattle of the cook's triangle should call the crew to supper. That whole scene, with the men lounging about the yard, would have had a deceptive appearance to any one not aware of the circumstances.

But the undercurrent of taut suspense ran through them all. And no triangle's clarion would end this, for Nat Fenwick had forgotten all about supper and was in the door of the cookshack, watching and waiting too.

At last, the drum of hoofs began and Rick knew the moment was nearing.

The eastward rim was in shadow now, the approaching horseman hard to distinguish. They were quite close before he could make out the big ewe-necked gray and the huge bulk of the man topping him.

Brag Nabor had to have a big horse, to carry up under his tremendous weight. Dismay touched Rick Thompson as he saw the Keystone ramrod, and he could understand now the cruel, secret amusement he had read in the anticipation of these other men.

Brag Nabor was a gunman, but probably he took more keen delight in a roughhouse, in getting those big slabs of hands onto another man's body and breaking and hurting him. If that was what he had ahead of him, Rick knew he stood small chance.

He didn't let any of these thoughts show, however. He did not even rise from the top step, but stayed seated where he was while the horseman pounded nearer. But under the growing sound he spoke softly to the girl, who had waited out this tense interval in a chair at the back of the veranda:

"Maybe you'd better go in the house."

It was all he said. And there was no sound from behind him, so he knew the girl had not moved.

The Keystone crew were on their feet, and Nat Fenwick was walking quickly forward from the cookshack door.

Brag Nabor reined in and the big gray braced itself against his weight as he swung a thick cowhide boot across the saddle, stepped down into the dust. The foreman's voice rang out in a throaty bellow across the stillness: "Damn, I mean I'm really hungry! Somebody brain a steer and lay him out on a platter—I'll eat 'im raw!"

One of his men stepped in quickly, spoke to his chief. A look of vacuity washed over the big man's ugly, bearded face. He swiveled for a sharp look at the slim shape of the man seated on the veranda steps, and his brow dragged down. He mumbled a question or two.

"Oh, he does?" he growled then, in a rising rumble. Suddenly he pushed the informer aside and, with the eyes of every man on him, waded across the yard to the steps.

He stopped at the foot of them, his cowhides planted wide apart and his little bullet-shaped head jutted forward. He was the ugliest man Rick Thompson thought he had ever seen.

For a moment no one spoke, as Rick sat looking down at the other, meeting his stare directly with a calmness that he was far from feeling.

Brag Nabor spat into the dust. Arms akimbo, big fists on hips, he shouted: "Well, here I am. Fire me!"

He was a head taller than Rick Thompson, maybe forty pounds heavier, and the sweaty shirt was stretched across the bulge of heavily muscled torso and shoulders. Looking at the size of the man, Rick sighed a little. "I suppose I can only try," he murmured.

Someone laughed, in the watching circle of men below in the yard.

From a corner of the porch old Nat Fenwick's dry voice rasped in the gathering dusk:

"Light's gettin' dim and so are my eyes, but this hogleg I'm carryin' has an uncanny way of shooting in the dark. Anybody tries to mix into

57

this uninvited, I may not work too hard to hold 'er in!"

No one answered him. Silence settled. In it Rick Thompson thought of the girl behind him, on the veranda, and wished again that she had stepped inside the house. He hated for her to witness what he knew was going to happen here.

He got up slowly, and moving very methodically he unhooked his gunbelt and laid holster and weapon aside. This seemed to strike Nabor as very amusing. "Really asking for it, aren't you?" he grunted, and with a harsh chuckle jerked his own belt from buckle and shucked his gun.

Rick Thompson, at the top of the steps, waited motionless until the big man was rid of the weapon. Then with a sudden movement he shot his arms out, put a hand against the roof support at either side of him and launched himself down the steps that way, feet first.

Sharp heeled boots caught Brag Nabor squarely in his thick chest and a grunt of lost wind burst from him; then they were both down in the dirt, in a tangle.

# CHAPTER VI

Thompson had landed heavily, his fall only partly broken by Nabor's thick frame. But he lay there only an instant, while the first shouts of the watching men burst and echoed in his ears. Then he scrambled away, got his feet under him.

Thick fingers seized an ankle, jerked him flat. And the whole weight of the big man was hurled upon his lower body, one great fist slashing in haymaker blows trying to connect with Thompson's face. They fell short; one slammed squarely into his belly, however, tearing the wind from him.

Writhing in agony, Rick Thompson somehow managed to let drive one bent knee, and luckily it took his opponent in the mouth and jerked his head around savagely. His weight rolled off, and the smaller man had a moment to fight wind back into his lungs, to combat the sickening effects of that belly blow.

He got clear to his feet this time, sobbing for breath, his limbs moving sluggishly as though weighted with lead. Brag Nabor was up too, shaking his bullet head, wiping a smear of blood onto his sleeve from smashed lips.

The yells of the watching men never ceased

now. They beat against Rick's hearing as he faced his opponent, half crouched. And Nabor came in at once, lunging with hands stretched to seize and break the other.

Rick ducked wildly to avoid that murderous grip. The hands missed his throat, but one caught a handful of shirt at Thompson's shoulder and Rick pivoted around on one heel, missed his footing and fell hard against Nabor. Then the shirt gave with a ripping of cloth. The sleeve ripped away and Thompson left it in Nabor's hand as he ducked clear.

Dancing away, he let drive a blow that caught the big man squarely in the battered mouth, and it must have hurt. Rick felt the smear of blood under his knuckles, the edge of a broken tooth. He swung with his left, connecting with the side of the ugly head; then he was clear.

Lumbering after him, Brag Nabor was not quite so eager now to plunge into a clinch. That first lunge of Thompson's down the steps, spike-heeled boots striking the chest of the man with all his weight behind them, must have hurt; so had the few telling blows Rick had put over since. But the big man was far from licked. He shook his head, cursing, and came in with great fists lashing.

For a moment Thompson stood to him, and the heavy slugging of fists made a sodden sound in the growing shadows pooled under the cottonwoods of the yard. Suddenly the watchers had fallen silent, seeing this thing settle down to a brutal slugging match, toe to toe, with Rick Thompson giving slowly before the greater bulk of his opponent.

Then a blow he missed left Thompson for a moment off balance, strung out, vulnerable—and with a grunt of satisfaction Brag Nabor brought a fist chopping down brutally against the point where his neck and shoulder joined.

Stunned, Rick fell back stumbling. Nabor followed eagerly, wicked light in his little eyes, hitting with both fists one after the other, to either side of the head. He forced the smaller man back and back, through swirling dust, toward the cluster of saddled horses beside the watering trough. At the violence, the noise, the scent of blood, those broncs were shying and dancing fearfully.

Suddenly Rick went down in a rolling sprawl directly beneath the hoofs of one of the mounts. Choking on dust, he scrambled madly to escape. One steel shoe caught him a numbing blow on the hip. He got away, lurched to his feet on the yonder side of the horse.

At the same moment Brag Nabor jabbed a hand viciously against the bronc's flank and sent the beast plunging sidewards, slamming into Rick Thompson. Already groggy, he was hurled bodily against another plunging animal. And before he could get free Brag Nabor was coming at him again through the thick confusion of hoofs and dust.

A hand gripped his shirt front, pulled him erect. Then Nabor's other fist smashed him and he went backpedalling helplessly. He was hardly conscious when he struck the edge of the water trough and hung there, weaving.

Against a shifting screen of dust he watched Brag Nabor, still coming at him. Horses scattered as the rest of the tough crew came running safely behind their leader, fanning out, following the fight across the yard. Rick thought he saw old Nat Fenwick, hobbling after the rest with fear and dismay printed in his face. And up on the porch, no doubt, Mary Jane Carlon was watching this bloody, ignominious beating . . .

Somehow he roused himself to a final effort. As the bulky shape of Nabor bore in he pushed away from the trough, staggering forward to meet him. He even unleashed a wavering right that didn't seem to have any steam in it. Nabor ducked that easily, and started a wide haymaker that would finish his opponent.

Rick Thompson twisted wildly to avoid that blow. His foot slipped in mud formed where water overflowed the horse trough. He went down in a sprawl, in cold mud. He took a hard kick from one of Nabor's heavy cowhides, and then the big man, carried by the impetus of his swing, stumbled over Thompson's prone shape. There was a heavy thud as he crashed against the side of the trough.

Thompson rolled, came to hands and knees. He saw Nabor floundering against the trough, stunned. With a shout tearing from his throat Rick leaped at the big man, full astride his back, and with all the strength remaining in him shoved Brag Nabor's head under the surface of the water and held it there.

Nabor fought and struggled under him like a bucking bronc, but Rick rode him with lips drawn back savagely across set teeth, arms set hard as he doubled the man across the edge of the trough. Their struggles lashed the water, drenched them both. But then, slowly, the violence began to die in big Nabor.

At last, wearily, Rick Thompson stepped back. It took all his strength to haul Nabor's torso out of the water and dump him, soggy and gasping, into the mud. He turned then, put his weight against the trough while he faced Brag Nabor's men. They were hauled up, staring in shocked disbelief.

Thompson pawed the hair out of his bloody, swollen face. "Get your warsacks," he panted, tiredly. "Collect what's due you from Miss Carlon—and ride." He added, remembering: "The one with the Keystone bronc will have to double up with somebody 'til you hit town. And somebody get this thing on its feet and ready to travel."

He indicated the gasping, half-drowned hulk of Brag Nabor, with a prod of his boot. Then he turned away from the men and went at a half-stagger toward the house, leaving Nat Fenwick and his Peacemaker to see that those orders were carried out.

On the veranda Mary Jane Carlon stood with horror in her pretty face. Rick stood at the bottom of the steps, looking up at her for a moment, torn and bruised and bloody, and drenched. He said thickly: "It wasn't nice to watch, I guess. I'm sorry. You can't always fight fair, against a brute . . ."

It was all he had the strength to say.

Later that evening, by the light of a kerosene lamp, the three sat together in the office with the ranch books and papers organized and piled neatly on the desk before them. A silence held in the musty little room. The story those papers told was not a pleasant one, and for the moment no one trusted himself to speak.

A reaction from the violence of the fight with Brag Nabor had settled over Rick Thompson. He had bathed, put on clean clothes, put court plaster on the worst cuts of his battered face. But he still felt drained of all strength, and a leaden weight sat upon his spirit.

Maybe it had something to do with the memory of that horror that had looked from the girl's eyes, as she stood staring down at him with the blood of battle on him. Nothing more had been said about the fight but he wondered what thoughts, what opinion of him lay now behind her thoughtful glance. Had he lowered himself, done permanent harm to her estimate of him, by that show of brutality?

He wondered, too, how it was that the opinion of this girl he had known for only a matter of a few hours should have become so all-important to him.

Old Nat Fenwick sat hunkered on a rawhide-bottom chair, glowering at nothing, sucking noisily on an ancient briar which he considerately refrained from firing up. "Well," he said, breaking a silence that had held too long, "what's the answer?"

"It looks very bad," Mary Jane answered him. "It looks as though I sold half interest in a ranch I hardly owned!" She swung a pleading look at Rick Thompson. "You must believe me—I had no idea the Keystone's affairs were in such a shape. I swear I didn't know about the note at the bank. I thought we were solvent; my uncle always claimed so, and—I don't know why—I just took his word for it!"

"Of course I believe you," Rick said quickly. "What we have to do now is figure out how we're going to get through the next months. All the cash capital we have is what's left in that wallet. As for the bank's note—" He leaned and took a letter from the desktop. "If we can locate the cattle to meet this shipping date that Ollie Pierce arranged, we'll be able to cover the interest payments and keep floating awhile."

"All it amounts to, then," Nat Fenwick finished drily, "is us doing the work of a nine-man crew, combing those breaks under the rim for enough head of prime beef to satisfy the buyer when he hits town next month. . . . Well, it's quite a spell since I choused a wild one out of the brush, but I guess it's never too late for an old dog to relearn old tricks!"

Mary Jane looked at the old man, in the yellow lamplight. She shook her head, and there were tears in her pretty eyes. "Nat," she began miserably, "I don't know what to say—"

Rick's sour mood gave him a sudden roweling and he shoved up from his chair, moved to stare sightlessly into the opaque darkness piled outside the opened window.

It looked hopeless, to him. He had thought they had a chance—until he saw the records of Keystone's finances. Now all he could think of was the misery in the eyes of Mary Jane Carlon; the dogged, hopeless loyalty of the old cook; and—the misplaced faith of three mossyhorn cowpunchers who had entrusted him with their life savings, only to have the money poured down a rathole that seemed to have no bottom.

It was at that moment he heard the beat of a single horse moving in across the night, drawing steadily toward the ranch buildings.

The others had caught the sound, too. "What do you suppose this is?" Old Nat Fenwick growled. "More trouble?"

Mary Jane carried the lamp as they all three went through the hall into the front part of the house. They heard the bronc clatter to a halt, and a moment later a heavy tread moving deliberately up the veranda steps. The girl exclaimed quickly: "That's my uncle—I know his step."

"And comin' here alone!" grunted the cook. "He's got more nerve than any other rat I ever knew."

A cheerful voice called through the screen: "Anybody home?" And without invitation Oliver Pierce swung open the door and entered the living room.

His hat was in his hand; lamplight picked out the reddish tint of his wiry hair, and the glint of a gold tooth behind his confident smile. His wide shape almost filled the doorway as he stood looking at the trio, and something made Mary Jane draw nearer to Rick and put one hand into the crook of his arm.

Then Pierce moved into the room, like a man thoroughly at home, and settled into a comfortable chair. He put the hat on his knees, steepled his fingers and looked across them at the three who still stood unspeaking.

"You don't look so good since this afternoon when I saw you," he observed, studying Rick's bruised and swollen face.

"I imagine you've seen Brag Nabor," old Nat growled from his station near the door. "He don't look so good either."

Rick Thompson cut in coldly: "Tell us what you want and get it over with. We're busy."

"Yes, I know," the older man agreed, nodding his sleek head. "I saw light in the office window as I rode in, and thought probably you were going through the desk. Ah—too late for these to do you any good, I suppose." He reached into a pocket of his coat, and lamplight shimmered from a small ring of keys as they jingled onto the table top beside Thompson. "I'm sure a little thing like a locked desk couldn't stop a resourceful gent like you."

"Keep talking," said Rick, eyes unswerving from the other man's face.

"I should think the books in the desk would have told you all you need to know. Now that you've found out something about this pig in a poke you've got yourself stuck with, maybe you'll be glad to listen to a little offer."

He leaned back in the chair, tilted his head to smile at the three people on their feet.

"Thompson, I don't take you for a fool. Given a chance to recoup some fraction at least of what you've lost if you stick to this proposition, I think you'll take it." He switched his glance to Mary Jane. "You, too, my dear. I'm willing to forget your ill treatment of me, and pay you cash for your share of Keystone. Say the word and I'll write a check before I leave tonight, and relieve you of all your worries—"

Rick Thompson, who ten minutes before had been in a mood to accept any way of escaping the hopeless setup at Keystone, heard himself saying now:

"Get on your feet and get off this ranch, Pierce! We'll battle this thing out to the finish, rather than let you take over Keystone for a fraction of its value. And what's more, don't give us any trouble or you might find a legal investigation afoot of the way this ranch has been mismanaged under your trusteeship, and allowed to slide to the brink of failure. That's just a little warning!"

It had Oliver Pierce on his feet, eyes blazing at the other man. Abruptly he turned on the heel of a polished boot and strode heavily to the door. He swung back, there, upon the three in the room.

"I'll take back what I said," he remarked crisply. "Perhaps you *are* a little of a fool, after all, Mr. Thompson. But at least it helps to know where we all stand." An ugly look spread across his features. "By the way, a very sad thing occurred in town this evening. Sam Hughes—"

A gasp broke from Mary Jane. Pierce went on, blandly:

"Someone seems to have entered the hotel and beat Hughes within an inch of his life. Robbery, obviously. He may not recover—doctor says a skull fracture."

Rick Thompson had trouble controlling the cold anger that tensed through him. "You keep your promises, don't you? Well, let's just watch and see if you're able to keep one or two you made to me, today. . . . Meanwhile, you filthy skunk, get on that bronc before I kick you on it!"

The screen door jangled behind Oliver Pierce's solid shape, and without another word the man was gone. It was a long time after the hoofbeats faded out, that Rick Thompson managed to quell the sickened fury within him.

Pierce and his men would pay, he swore silently, for their cruel retaliation against the little hotel keeper. That at least, was one promise he personally meant to see fulfilled!

# CHAPTER VII

Nat Fenwick slept on a cot in the eatshack; so, his first night on Keystone, Rick had the big bunkhouse to himself. The crew had left it in a messy litter of discarded clothing, tattered magazines and dirt. It took him the good part of an hour to get it swept and cleaned up decently, with the doors and windows propped open to air the sweaty, horsey stench out of the place.

Despite the tiredness of his thrashed body, it took him a long time to get to sleep. With all that he had on his mind to trouble him he lay well past midnight in the bunk he had chosen for himself, smoking in the darkness and going over the treadmill of the day's events and the problems of the immediate future.

Seven hundred head. Gathering them in the time limit granted under the terms of that buyer's letter would be a terrific, back breaking task—certainly, with no one to handle the chore but a man, a girl, and an old rheumatic ranch cook who hadn't dabbed a loop or put a cowpony through its paces in a dozen years. . . .

He would have to ride for Willow Crossing, first thing in the morning. There was no other answer. Keystone had to have at least a couple extra riders, for the time being anyway.

With gray dawn he was up and pulling on his clothes. Automatically he reached for gun and belt, had them around his flat waist when, remembering, he hesitated. Then with a grim shake of the head he stripped them off and hung them back on the nail. Much as he disliked riding into Ollie Pierce's town unarmed, there was no sense inviting trouble by flouting the no-gun ordinance of which Vince Kirby had warned him yesterday. Wearing a gun would give his enemies too good an excuse to bring a fight against him openly.

The girl was not yet up, but a pencil of smoke lifted from the chimney of the eatshack. Nat Fenwick, nearly doubled over with rheumatism, was pottering around and banging pans on the stove as Thompson entered; he returned Rick's greeting with a sour nod.

"I ain't as bad off as I look," he added, shrugging bent shoulders. "It allus takes me half the morning to get my joints workin' smooth. . . . And how's *your* health, after that little go-around with Brag Nabor?"

"Pretty sore," Thompson admitted.

"Ain't to be wondered at, way you gents was hittin' each other with hosses and things." The cook used a poker on his fire, shoved in a chunk of pinewood. He grumbled: "Can't get the damn stove hot—"

Rick Thompson said, "I don't want much

breakfast to speak of. A cup of coffee, if you've got some made. I'll be riding, pronto."

Nat gave him a quick look. "To town?" He scowled in disapproval as he got a china cup off its hook, filled it from the big pot that simmered on the back of the stove. Thompson drank it standing up, explaining his mission between gulps. "Good java," he said, and upending his empty cup on the drainboard nodded again to old Nat and left the eatshack on his way to the corral.

Behind him he heard the cook's sudden exclamation: "Hey, wait a minute! *Where's your gun?*" But he did not slow his stride.

The heat was already coming into the day when he rode into Willow Crossing, forking his bay gelding with the livery stable bronc trailing. Morning freshness lay on the town, turning its dust to powdered gold, flashing brightness from the surface of the creek and the steel rails that crossed it on their high trestle. Thompson rode to the livery first of all, turned the rented horse over to the day hostler and paid his bill.

"Some excitement at the hotel last night, I understand," he remarked by way of conversation.

The hostler gave him a look but made no answer. Thompson rode on along the street, maintaining an alert caution and watching the people he saw on the wooden sidewalk. He missed the familiar weight of belt and gun about his hips, he wanted to finish his business and be done with this town, and with the nervous tightening it put into the muscles of his back.

But when he came abreast of the hotel something made him put his gelding to the tiepole there. Broken glass crunched underfoot as he crossed the walk and went up the broad steps. The big plate glass windows had been smashed; when he stepped through the doorway he saw grim evidence of the havoc wreaked here last night and it turned his dark face bleak with anger.

Chairs and other furnishings were in splinters, the upholstering of the sofa slashed and springs and stuffing ripped out. The pigeonholed rack had been torn down from the wall behind the desk, papers and ledgers were scattered over the worn carpet. A skinny youngster with dustpan and broom was trying to clean up some of the mess; he looked up with quick fear showing in his eyes as he heard Thompson's step.

"Where's Sam Hughes?" Rick Thompson demanded. His voice was unintentionally harsh and the boy retreated a step, shaking his head.

"Please!" the youngster begged. "Leave him alone, can't you? What's my Pop ever done to—"

"I'm sorry, kid," Thompson said quickly. "I don't mean him any harm. I'm sort of a friend of his; and I heard he was in trouble. I'd like to see him, if there's no objections."

Mollified, the boy told him heavily; "He's over

74

at the doc's house. But I don't think he can talk to you, Mister. He's awful bad . . ."

Rick stayed long enough to help the youngster right some of the heavy furniture, and to ask some questions about the attack on his father. But the lad had not been at the hotel when it happened and if he knew or suspected anything was much too frightened to talk. Thompson learned from him the location of the doctor's house, and leaving the hotel stepped up to saddle and rode there, a smoldering anger inside him.

The doctor's place was a neat little cottage on the edge of town—the medico himself, a spare little man whose nearsighted eyes blinked at Thompson from behind thick glasses. He listened to the stranger's request, then shrugged and spread his hands in a small gesture. "Sure. You can see him—but it won't do you much good."

He took Rick into a neat, yellow-curtained bedroom. It was hard to believe the cocoon-like thing in the bed there was a man. Almost nothing of Sam Hughes' face was visible behind the bandages that covered it; he lay like one dead, and the doctor muttered sourly at Thompson's elbow:

"A fractured skull—somebody slammed him with a gunbutt, I think. He hasn't regained consciousness and it's less than a fifty-fifty chance that he will."

"Do all you can for him," said Thompson,

feeling sick inside. "And if he could come out of it enough to talk—"

"I'll know what to do!" the doctor promised tightly. "I'd give anything to be able to nail this on the thugs who did it. There were no witnesses at all."

"Kind of strange, isn't it?" said Rick. "A hotel lobby would seem like a pretty public sort of place."

The doctor shrugged. "Most folks would look the other way at a time like that, I suppose." His nearsighted eyes behind their thick lenses were on Thompson's face and he said suddenly: "Not changing the subject, but what was it you tangled with—a threshing machine? I'll take a look at those bruises if you want."

"No, thanks," said Rick shortly, and left.

He couldn't get the silent, beaten shape of the little hotel keeper out of his mind. If Sam Hughes could only talk, only hang the guilt on the men who had done that to him—but, even so, that wouldn't touch the one who had sent those marauders to the hotel. Legally, there was no way to link Oliver Pierce with this cruel punishment that Hughes had drawn upon himself, by his audacity in aiding Mary Jane Carlon against her uncle's plans.

The course of these dark thoughts was interrupted suddenly when sight of a trio of dusty cowponies, racked in front of the Lady Luck, called Rick Thompson's attention again to the main purpose of his journey to town this morning.

They were trailstained, with blanket rolls and warsacks and brush-scarred chaps strapped behind the saddles. Obviously, the property of some drifting cowhands, and that was the type rider Rick Thompson was looking for to help out on Keystone. He put his gelding to the rack and stepped down, swung under the pole, took the steps leading up to the batwing doors of the saloon.

As soon as they parted under his shoving hand he saw the owners of the horses—three dusty, nondescript figures in pushed-back sombreros, spurs at the heels of their rundown boots, drinks in front of them as they lined the mahogany exchanging small talk with the woodenlegged barkeep. Except for these the big room was empty. Morning sunlight fell across the sawdust-littered floor, and Rick Thompson's shadow blotted this out briefly as he pushed through the swinging doors and approached the bar.

He received brief nods from the three cow-hands, and from the aprons a stare that held on Thompson's battered face. The man remembered him from yesterday, and it looked like he had also heard something of what this stranger had done since hitting Willow Crossing. Could be he was a friend of Oliver Pierce.

Rick met his look coldly and ordered a drink. "Fill 'em up for these gents too, while you're at it," he said. The men nodded their thanks, and one invited him to share a round. "My limit," he said, shading his head with a smile. And after some small talk and comments on the weather: "You gents just trailing through, or would you maybe be interested in a job?"

The three exchanged glances and the one next to Thompson, who seemed to be the spokesman, allowed that such might be the case. "We got no plans," he said. "We'll be wanting to hitch on somewheres, eventually, and if you know of a good spot we wouldn't be hostile towards it."

"I'm in a tight," Rick told them, "and I need a few riders mighty bad—and quick. Regular pay, and decent grub. Okay?"

He saw the face of the bartender working as though the man had a tic. The aprons cleared his throat hoarsely. "Uh, gents—" he began. If he was trying to stick in a warning against signing on with Keystone, Thompson didn't wait for it. He added: "Soon as you're ready to travel we can be heading for the ranch."

The leader said, "Sure. All right with me," and they tossed their drinks off quickly. But as they turned to leave the batwings swung open suddenly and four men entered. Thompson recognized them all as part of the crew he had fired last evening at Keystone. And in the van, Brag

Nabor hauled up scowling blackly as he caught sight of Rick Thompson.

A cold finger touched Rick's spine, remembering he was unarmed. He saw the filled holsters of Brag Nabor and his men, saw the way big Nabor's hand twitched and jerked near the forward-jutting handle of his rubber-butted gun. The three cowhands Rick had just hired were armed but they did not look like gunfighters, nor did they know the danger building here; puzzlement was plain in them as they halted beside Rick, uncertainly.

Squared off, facing Brag Nabor, the man from Keystone waited for the other to make the first move.

# CHAPTER VIII

For a long moment a heavy silence built up, broken only by the tick of a banjo clock on the wall behind the bar. Then Brag Nabor's thick shoulders lifted, and a nasty sneer twisted his bearded mouth. "You, huh? Where's your gun, Thompson?"

Brag showed the effects of yesterday's fight as clearly as Rick. One eye was almost swollen shut, and there was a dark red scab across one cheek. Brag Nabor would never forgive this man who had beaten him in a rough-and-tumble. Rick knew that; knew Brag Nabor would always be waiting for a chance to even that score.

He said with icy humor: "My gun's at home, Brag. There's an ordinance against wearing them in this town—or so Vince Kirby tried to tell me yesterday. But maybe the law only applies to people that Ollie Pierce don't happen to like."

The big man snorted. "You're a coward, Thompson. That's why you ain't packin' an iron. You're a yellow, sneakin' coward that's scared of a fair fight."

Despite himself, Rick felt the angry blood begin to course into his face. "Give me a gun now, Brag," he said tightly. "Or lay your own aside—whichever way you want it. If you still need proof, after what I did to you yesterday—"

But perhaps Brag Nabor was not yet quite ready to tangle with this stranger for the second time. For he ignored the challenge, and let his ugly glance slide away from Thompson and take in the three strange cowhands who stood beside him, with bewildered looks on their sunburnt faces.

"Who's your friends?" he demanded.

The bartender answered him—unnecessarily. There was something mean in his voice as he said: "They just hired on with Keystone, Brag."

"Oh, they did?"

Slowly, deliberately, Nabor paced forward and halted in front of one of the trio, and the man backed away a little until the edge of the bar was against his spine. He looked uncomfortable under Brag Nabor's hard stare, and once he made a motion toward his gun but let the hand drop again, empty.

Brag Nabor said heavily: "You don't really think you want a job with that outfit, do you, friend?"

"I dunno why not," the other replied, stubbornly. But there was no conviction in his tone, and his glance shifted nervously as he saw Nabor's companions spreading out, closing in on the bar.

Rick Thompson snapped: "Cut it out, Brag! I'm warning you!"

The big man gave him only a flick of a glance, the edge of a contemptuous grin. And then without warning his huge fist came clubbing in a sharp, hard arc and the cowhand facing him reeled back against the bar, blood springing from a smashed lip.

Unarmed as he was, Rick Thompson started for Brag but the hard boring of a gun against his side hauled him up. One of Nabor's men had got to him quickly, and other drawn weapons were menacing the pair of cowhands who had moved to help their friend. White of face, they looked at the guns and turned their stares on Brag. One blurted out, "What the hell—!"

"I'm just convincing your friend that he don't want to hire on with Keystone," grunted Brag Nabor; and then the savage pleasure of inflicting pain glittered in his little eyes as he swung a second time, a third.

Helpless under the boring of that gunmuzzle into his body, Rick Thompson had to stand and see that punishment administered. But it did not last long. With the third blow the cowhand was hurled clear around; he sagged at the knees, eyes glazing, and made a feeble clutch at the edge of the slick mahogany as he went down in a limp heap. He struck the brass railing, rolled over on his back so that his unconscious, bloody face was turned up toward the shaft of sunlight across the batwings.

Almost reluctantly, Brag Nabor stepped back opening his huge fists, spreading the fingers. "I'm still looking for an argument," he said, turning his ugly grin on the other two cowhands. "I say you're not working for this gent. I say you're gonna pick up your friend and ride on about your business. How about it?"

The two exchanged glances. They carefully avoided looking at Rick Thompson. Without a word they got their hurt friend between them and carried him from the saloon. As the batwings swished to a halt the ragged sound of hoofbeats began and Rick Thompson saw them head out, one riding on either side to support the hurt man as he reeled and sagged in his saddle.

Then they were gone; and Rick knew they would keep going, putting this town and range well behind them. For they were only ordinary punchers, without the will or the incentive to stand up and fight in a battle that was none of their own.

His shoulders lifted on a slow, deep breath, and with fists hard clenched Thompson turned on Brag Nabor. "You filthy dog!" he said thickly. "Why take it out on a gent that never did anything to you?"

But they were leaving, without even a look for him. They trooped out of the Lady Luck and there was something scornful in the unhurried way they did it, not even waiting to hear what

Rick had to say. Anger beat strongly in him and he wished for his gun. Yet, alone, any reprisal he attempted would probably have meant quick death against the guns of that hard foursome— and such a form of suicide would be meaningless, gaining nothing.

He caught the woodenlegged barkeep's empty stare, turned away and strode out of the saloon. On the steps he surveyed the dusty street, wondering in some futility what his next move should be. Across the way he saw Nabor and the others bunched under the shadow of a wooden arcade, watching him—also waiting to see what he would do next.

Down at the foot of the long street the red roof of the depot shimmered in high morning sun. Rick went down the saloon steps, mounted again and rode slowly down there. At the agent's window he leaned from saddle and called in to the old man: "Any answer to that telegram I sent yesterday?"

"Not a word," the baldheaded man told him. Frowning, Rick Thompson digested this; for it was not what he had expected. Then, with a shrug, he thanked the old man and reined away. He was drawing a blank this morning, at every turn. And the single cup of coffee he had taken out at Keystone was leaving him now with a starved feeling inside him—but he didn't think any food he might eat in this town would sit well in his stomach. He couldn't head back for Keystone, though, without at least another effort at hiring the men he needed.

In front of the post office a string of whittling, tobacco-chewing loafers caught his eye. They were watching him with an acute and narrow interest and when he turned his bronc's head in their direction the group suddenly split apart. Some of the men suddenly thought of business elsewhere and moved away, quickly. Others turned their backs on him. Rick Thompson's jaw hardened bleakly as he guessed the truth: Nowhere in this town was he going to find men willing to hire on with Keystone, at any wages. The warning had got around, and with Brag Nabor and his gang of toughs to give it backing, it had had its effect.

At this bleak point in his thinking another horseman fell in beside him and he lifted his head sharply, saw the cold features of Hank Brush. Oliver Pierce's gunman gave him a nod and said, pleasantly: "Hiring hands, Thompson?"

"What do you want?" snapped Rick. He saw a twisted smile touch the other's lips beneath its clipped mustache, and then a gun was in Brush's hand and slanted at him across the saddlehorn.

"I want you to ride along with me," said Brush. "Just to the edge of town."

Rick said: "Running me out, are you? Why don't you leave that kind of a job for the brave marshal—or is Vince Kirby hiding out today?"

"Go on!" Brush ordered, and sunlight glinted as he gestured with the gun barrel. "Start riding."

They went up the street, and alternating bands of light and shadow poured across them as the sun kept pace beyond the buildings at their right hand. When they passed the last of the houses and the open trail stretched northward, Brush pulled in.

"All right," he said. "Get going. And count yourself lucky that you're getting off as easy as you have.

"I know Oliver Pierce, and I can tell you he ain't taking much more off you. I can also tell you that you'll do no good crying for help from anybody, or wasting your time trying to hire anyone to ride for you. Keystone is sunk. Nothin' was ever more certain than that!"

Rick Thompson said coldly, "Ollie Pierce is pretty damn sure of himself, isn't he? He thinks he's dug in so solid nobody can ever chase him out!"

"This range *is* Pierce!" Brush retorted sharply, beginning to lose his temper. "Nothin's gonna change that—not even this damn syndicate that's backing you!"

"Syndicate?" echoed Thompson, blankly.

He saw something strange then. He saw Hank Brush turn suddenly red and stammering, and all at once the gunman had stabbed his sixgun into holster and whirling his mount spurred away, to be swallowed up by the streets and buildings of the town. For a long moment Rick sat saddle where he was, utter puzzlement in him as he stared after the gunman.

"Syndicate?" he repeated, under his breath. "Now what in the world would he—"

And then realization came. That telegram! Oliver Pierce must have got hold of a copy, and had misinterpreted Rick's mention in it of "the Pool." The thought struck Rick Thompson as hilariously funny. "Wait 'til Montana and the boys find out they're a syndicate now!" he exclaimed, laughing aloud. But he sobered immediately.

He spoke to his bronc and let it out at a comfortable pace, trailing back to Keystone. He had accomplished absolutely nothing by this trip to Willow Crossing—except, indeed, to get an innocent stranger mauled by Brag Nabor's bruising fists. Yet, at that, he had learned a few things. For one, that Oliver Pierce had an ear in at the telegraph office! Thanks to Hank Brush's slip of the tongue he would know now that it was impossible to send a wire out of Willow Crossing without his enemy becoming aware of its contents. Which was something worth remembering!

Moreover, if Pierce thought there was the power of a syndicate somewhere in the background it would probably explain why he was holding off. His control of Willow Crossing was so complete that it would have been an easy matter for him to dispose of Thompson that morning—unarmed as he was, and with the town filled with Pierce's own gunmen. Such an open move, however, would have been too dangerous a bid for retaliation by the power backing Rick Thompson.

But now supposing Oliver Pierce discovered—as he was bound to eventually—that the "syndicate" that had him so worried consisted of three old, saddle-broken cowprods who, for a joke, liked to style themselves "the Mossyhorn Pool"—?

It would be no holds barred, after that! When that day came, Pierce would move against those who had defied his rule; and with his wealth and his hired guncrew, and the added weight of corrupt local law behind him, there would be small hope of standing against him!

# CHAPTER IX

But Rick Thompson did not ride directly to the ranch. Determined to try every possibility—and, furthermore, to test the real strength of Oliver Pierce's hold on this range—he made a wide sweep through the valley, riding in on the ranches that dotted its wide expanse and talking with their owners. He covered a lot of miles, from the eastern rim to the broken hills country at the west. He saw a lot of good graze, and thousands of cattle drifting and feeding under the sun-bright sky. But nowhere could he find support for Keystone in its lone-hand fight against Pierce.

Of the men he talked with—on ranch house verandas, beside dust-clouded branding corrals, on the seat of a wagon stretching wire around a deep, wind-stirred vega—one or two showed evidences of bad conscience. Thompson could sense this in their mumbled words, in the way their eyes sought the horizon and would not look squarely into his own. These men knew he was right, and standing aside and watching Oliver Pierce have his way against a girl like Mary Jane Carlon was a thing galling to their pride. But none stood ready to offer help, and thus call the wrath of Pierce upon his own head.

For too much of this land and the cattle grazing

it already carried the mark of Pierce's brand and his power. That was the whole situation.

". . . So it's up to us," Rick told Nat Fenwick and the girl later, as he finished recounting for them the results of his morning's efforts. "Looks like we got it alone. But, doggone it! We aren't licked until we've tried!"

Seven hundred head of prime beef. Half wild critters that the Keystone crew under Brag Nabor had let run untended, in the brushy breaks below the red sandstone rim, until they were almost more than a man and a trained cowhorse could handle.

Rick Thompson had known the whole weight of the job would fall upon his own shoulders, because his two helpers—heartbreakingly willing though they were to hold up their end of the task—simply could not fill the place of hard-handed, agile young cowprods. He accepted this. He took to the saddle at gray dawn and he stuck there until fatigue dragged him out of it late at night.

He drove himself mercilessly, to fight the thorny brush and the fleetfooted cattle that snaked through it, avoiding his rope, trickily dodging past him and heading back into the familiar gullies and thickets when he tried to head them off, shove them down to join the slowly-growing gathers.

More than once a cornered steer would turn

on him, charge insanely in a mad try to gore the persecuting bronc and rider that blocked his path of escape into the chaparral growth. At such times he faced a gamble with death itself, when a misstep on the stony earth could have felled his scrambling cowpony and thrown the rider hard against impaling horns, under sharp, trampling hoofs.

Somehow he always came out of it, but the narrowness of his escapes left him limp, wrung out, with sweat streaking his face and soaking blackly the armpits of his dusty shirt. Then a cussing helped—unless he thought of the girl, who at that moment could be risking her own neck in just such a perilous spot.

Mary Jane came to know when he had been in one of those tight moments, because he always came to her afterward with warnings to greater caution. "You've got to stop taking chances," he told her fiercely, leaning to accept the steaming cup of coffee she handed up to him—those days he even ate, whenever he did, in saddle. "This ain't a job for you. Between you and that little pony, there's not enough combined weight to throw against one of these brush-crazy mavericks!"

She only smiled up, tiredly, into his gaunted face with its hollow eyes and beardstubbled cheeks streaked with sweat and dirt. "I only do my share," she told him quietly. "If you can give what you have to the job, Rick Thompson, I have a right to do what I can. And just look at Nat Fenwick—"

The old cook was, indeed, an inspiring sight as he forced himself into saddle again and rode to combat the wild ones and the aches of his own tired body. They had moved camp out from the ranch headquarters, with a packhorse laden with food and supplies enough to last. In the mornings old Nat was the first out of his bedroll, doing the chores when he wasn't riding and disgruntled because the girl insisted on helping with the beans and sourdough biscuits. He cussed every-thing—his tortured joints, the firewood, the wild brush cattle. But he never wavered in his loyalty to the iron he had ridden and potwrangled for, twenty years and longer.

A week of this, under the double burden of fatigue and pressure of time, and the three were turning gaunted and sunblackened, their tempers worn to an edge.

They didn't talk very much. Tired as they were, talking only led to sharp and hasty words, and then to bitter self reproach at the thought of having hurt one another's feelings. But the work was going forward. In certain blind pockets whose open ends they cut off with rope and pole fences, small gathers of cattle were accumulating, their numbers growing steadily and as fast as a man and a girl and an old cripple could chouse the big red steers into the pens. It began to look as though they might yet have their herd collected before the day that delivery was scheduled into the shipping pens at Willow Crossing.

Then, one hazy, blistering morning, Rick Thompson came pushing a couple of steers toward one of these improvised holding pens and found someone had torn the crude fence down, and let forty head of beef vanish into nowhere.

He hauled up and sat for a long minute, blankly staring. He had expected this to happen. There was no way to guard the several collecting points and it had been too much to hope that Oliver Pierce, presented with such a painless opportunity of nullifying their labors and preventing them from meeting the delivery date, should have passed it up. But he had gone on, hoping for the best, and now the worst had happened.

Hoof-torn ground showed how those two-score head of cattle had bolted to freedom over the wreckage of the fence. There were tracks of horses, too—a pair of riders. Even boot-marks at one place where one of the men had dismounted briefly to work on the fence. The tracks were very fresh. Likely the mischief had been done about the time when gray dawn was melting into day. Three hours ago, perhaps.

With his eye he followed the course the cattle had taken, back toward the tumbled breaks. To serve Pierce's aim, all that was necessary would be to haze the critters into the chaparral and turn them loose there, leaving the hardpressed trio at Keystone the chore of gathering them again. The damage would be done already, the forty steers scattered to hell and gone through the brush. They would be even charier and harder to corral, a second time.

But then another thought put a frown on Thompson's sun-blackened features, as he raised his eyes to the red rim lifting directly before him. There were breaks in the solid wall of that rampart, and it could be the stolen cattle had been headed for one of those. Maybe the idea was to rustle them across the wall, not merely to scatter them; and if that was the case, the picture would be entirely different.

He knew two riders would have slow going and a damned tough time, keeping those forty wild ones on the trail, preventing them from bolting for the thickets. The missing beef wouldn't have got far in any three hours. . . .

Faint as it was, it was a chance worth looking to. Without another moment's hesitation Thompson gave his bay the spurs and took after the hoof-torn trail.

When he kept getting farther into the breaks and the sign still held ahead of him, his hopes lifted. There was plenty of evidence to show where the riders had worked hard to keep their charges from breaking for the chaparral. It looked as though they had their hands full. And Rick Thompson, pressing forward over the clearly marked and climbing trail, knew he was gaining rapidly. With luck he might even overtake his quarry before the cattle thieves reached the notch in the rim, and the open country beyond where they would be able to make better time.

It was characteristic of him that he didn't give much thought to what would happen if he did catch up with that pair. Two against one. There could be worse odds, and Rick Thompson was too angry to care. The patience that had carried him through a week of punishing toil was snapped now and he was ready to take his mad out on somebody—anybody.

The brush, more than shoulder-high to his gelding, reduced visibility almost to nothing. But this fell back as he mounted to the rim. A small wind moved down at him through the notch and on it he caught the sour tang of dust. It meant he was hard on the stolen stock now and he pushed forward eagerly; though the cattle thieves would top the rim before he caught up with them, they would not be far in the lead.

He came into the gap—the merest knife-slit break in the crumbling sandstone. The floor of the fissure tilted upward sharply, and he had almost reached the higher level when a slight twist in the trail brought him head-on into a lashing rifle bullet.

Pulling back sharply, he backed his mount in behind the protection of a bulging wall and held it there, listening tensely. Echoes of the shot bounced away within the narrow notch, and a cloud of quartz dust kicked up by the bullet sparkled in the air a moment, then was whipped away by the faint breeze. Silence returned, and stillness.

Rick Thompson was safe here from lead, but also he was pinned down and held helpless. He knew now he had ridden into a trap, and that one or both of the cattle thieves must be waiting ahead there for another chance at him. That he was still alive he owed entirely to the impatience of the ambusher, who had opened up before he came well into the sights and thus given him a chance to get back into cover.

He looked at the wall rising above his head, slapped the grainy rock with one hand. Rotten, crumbling stuff, its surface very much eroded by wind and water seepage. Its condition gave him his cue.

The rifle in Thompson's saddleboot had no sling. He fashioned one quickly from his rope, with loops about stock and muzzle, and slung the weapon across his shoulders. A stout scrub oak thrust out from the wall just above his head. Standing in the saddle, he tested his weight against this and then hauled himself up.

Here he was only a half dozen feet from the top

of the fissure. He went up, inch by inch, finding hand and toe holes in the crumbling sand. When he dragged himself over the lip of the wall he lay prone there for a long minute, getting his breath and listening for any sounds.

Atop the rim the wind was strong, the sun's beat no less intense than below on Keystone graze. It was rolling, wild, barren range. Raising up to hands and knees, he quickly sighted a small cup below him spotted with the shapes of thirty or forty head of cattle. And he knew at once they were the missing stock, and that the mounted figure riding herd on them was one of those he was after.

Even as he looked the horseman, who had been peering toward the notch in obvious concern, suddenly put his bronc around and came away from the herd at a fast lope, laying out a streamer of dust behind him. Thompson ducked quickly, though he didn't think he had been seen. The horseman was pulling to the right, toward the spot where Rick knew the busher had lain to take his shot.

Cautiously Rick Thompson reached back and drew his saddle gun over his head, got it into position and levered a cartridge into the breech. The rider was out of his line of vision by that time, somewhere in the rocks below and in front of him. He came up again cautiously, and began working forward with rifle balanced in right hand, being careful to allow no scrape of boots or clothing across the sandy rock.

He made for a thin screen of buckbrush, found that just beyond the ground fell away. As he held up a moment he heard voices:

"Damn you for a bungler, nohow, Pecos! I dunno why I team up with you. You had every chance in the world to get the guy."

"Lemme alone, Red! Mebbe I did get him. Ain't seen hide or hair of him since, have we?"

Thompson poked his rifle barrel out, parted the brush as far as he dared. At once he saw them, on their bellies in the little pit below him, talking close together and peering over into the silent mouth of the notch. Their backs were turned to him. It couldn't have been simpler, and he didn't even need to have brought the rifle.

He got to his feet. "Waiting for somebody, fellows?" he asked quietly.

It was really astonishing, the scramble that ensued. The pair below him began to squirm as though prodded with a redhot poker, trying to get around. One even got a sixgun into his fingers but when he saw the rifle muzzle full on him he let it go as though it burned him. For a moment they lay there, staring at him in astonishment and fear.

"Gawd!" one of them croaked.

Strangely enough, they weren't any of Brag Nabor's tough crew. They looked to Thompson like a couple of range tramps—as sorry a pair as he had laid eyes on in some time. They were bearded, in wreckage of clothing and rundown boots and shapeless headgear. He saw their horses now, tied in brush some yards away. These had patched saddles and gear hung together with baling wire. One of the rigs was a rimfire hull that somehow stuck to the rattailed nag on a single cinch.

More than a little puzzled, Rick said crisply: "You by the rifle—give it a good, hard kick. Both of you shed any guns you may be wearing, and then get to your feet."

As they obeyed, slowly, he leaped down into the tiny pit, keeping his saddle gun ready. One of the pair was taller than Rick, blackbearded and skinny and with a hang dog look about him. That must be the one he had heard called "Pecos," the one who had tried the shot at him and failed; because the other, smaller man had fiery red hair and beard stubbles. Even his eyebrows were thick and red, and his round face was burnt the color of brick.

"Well, what's the deal?" snapped Rick Thompson, into the silence that piled up as his prisoners stood scowling at him and his rifle. "How come Pierce would pick a couple of scarecrows like you for this job? Was it that he didn't want his own men involved?"

The beanpole, Pecos, tried to look ignorant.

"Never heard of nobody named Pierce," he grunted.

"Oh, the hell with it!" Red snorted, scornfully. "This guy knows the score. Why cover up for anybody?"

"He did hire you, then?"

"For five bucks apiece. We was to watch our chance to run off some steers, and put you outa mischief if we could get a good shot."

Rick Thompson shook his head. "Pretty small pay for that kind of a job, I'd figure."

The one called Pecos butted in, with wounded pride: "We was to keep the steers, too. I'll have you know we ain't no cheap skates!"

"Shut up!" growled Red. His eyes sullenly on Thompson, he said: "You're dealin' the deck, Mister. What game are you calling for?"

Thompson studied the disreputable pair for a long moment. Then he said, abruptly: "How would you like to go to work?"

Stunned beyond words, they only stared at him through a long slow tick of the clock. Then Pecos said, hoarsely, "You're funnin'!"

"The position I'm in," Rick answered him, "I can't waste time on jokes. . . . How many of those forty head did you boys lose, pushing them up through the breaks?"

"Why—none," said Red, rusty brows dragging down in a puzzled frown.

"That's as I figured—which in my language

means you must be a ringtailed pair of buckaroos, and no mistake! Well, Keystone needs riders, and I can't be particular where I get them. You want to sign on, I'll give you a try. Regular wages."

"But—Keystone!" exclaimed the lanky Pecos, his stare widening. "We was told—"

This time his partner silenced him with an elbow hard against his bony ribs. "The hell with what we was told!" he said, fiercely. "This guy's givin' us a break, see? He's got us dead to rights, but if he's willing to forget what we set out to do to him, we're gonna play along.

"You've got you a pair of hands, Mister," he told Rick. "I'm Red Morse, and this is Pecos— uh—what's your last name, Pecos?"

"Hell, I ain't even got a fust name," the tall saddletramp grunted. "I never had no mammy nor no pappy."

"Just picked you up in the cowlot, huh?" snorted the redhaired one. "Well, when do we start to work, Mister?"

"As of right now," said Rick, grinning faintly. There was something about this derelict pair that he liked, despite the fact that they had stolen from him and that the tall Pecos' rifle chamber still held the spent shell with which the man had tried to kill him—for a five dollar bill!

He couldn't trust them. He pegged them as a completely amoral pair of range bums with only the most rudimentary code of conduct, and with neither pity, conscience, or fear of hellfire. But they knew cattle and he was determined to get some good out of that knowledge, for the sake of the desperate Keystone iron.

"First off," he said crisply, "we're chousing those steers back where you got 'em. You boys are going to do the work—I'll ride behind with my rifle handy and see that you behave yourselves. I'll keep these irons of yours, too, until I get an idea it's safe to let you have them back.

"My horse is down there in the notch below us. Go get him for me, Red."

"Go get him, Pecos," Red relayed the order, with another elbow jab.

Pecos climbed morosely into the saddle that had the missing cinch, and clattered away. While Rick Thompson collected the firearms of the pair, Red nonchalantly fished out a piece of chaw, picked pocket lint off it and offered it to the other. Rick refused, and Morse helped himself to a jawful. He had quickly recovered from all astonishment at this turn of events; and when a few minutes later, the three were mounted and moving down on the cattle to turn them back into the notch and down off the rim, he was already calling Rick "Boss" with great familiarity. The gloomy Pecos forked his bony nag and said absolutely nothing.

A strange pair; but though he kept a careful eye

on them Rick Thompson allowed himself to hope that they would fill a need. Two more hands for Keystone! Even such as they were, they almost doubled the strength of that embattled little crew.

# CHAPTER X

Two days later Sam Hughes, the hotelman, was buried in Willow Crossing's Boothill. He had died in the night from his beating, never once recovering sufficiently to name the men who had killed him.

Nat Fenwick brought the news back to Keystone, when he rode into town for the mail and to see if there had yet been any answer to the telegram Rick Thompson sent the day of his arrival. There wasn't any. This puzzled Rick, who had expected his wire to bring the three old punchers of the "Mossyhorn Pool" scooting hell for leather to see the ranch he had bought into for them. Their nonappearance had him a little worried.

And Mary Jane, he could see, was hard hit by the word of the hotelman's dying. She blamed herself, he knew; nothing he was able to say could shake her conviction that it was due solely to her that poor Sam Hughes had met such a dreadful and violent end. She wanted at least to attend the funeral; and as things were progressing well since Red and Pecos joined the Keystone crew Thompson took the time to accompany her, leaving Nat Fenwick in charge of things at the ranch.

This time, he wore his gun. He had gained nothing at all by leaving it behind, the last time he ventured into Oliver Pierce's stronghold; and with the girl along he didn't dare to be without the means of protecting her. Let Vince Kirby take exception, if he liked!

Rick Thompson had no fear of the gunhawk— nor had he left, now, any part of his old respect for Kirby's reputation. That was as dead as all the rest of Willow Crossing's lurid past. . . .

The clear warm weather still held. A few lazy clouds hung above the sandstone rim but they didn't mean rain. The man and the girl talked little as they rode across the rolling range; they were both worn and tired from the hard labor of the past week, and Rick Thompson respected his companion's mood.

He studied her profile, noticing with a frown how events were wearing on her, fining her down. He himself had lost pounds of weight, and his mirror when he shaved showed him a sun-blackened face that must be turning near as gaunt as that of the saddletramp, Pecos.

A small crowd was already collecting down at the cemetery. They rode without incident through the town, past the hotel and the Lady Luck, past the depot and shipping pens and on to where Boothill lay athwart the south trail. There had been no challenge, no sign of Brag Nabor or his crew. Rick Thompson helped Mary

Jane down from saddle, took her arm as they moved quietly among the gravestones to where a preacher's voice already intoned solemnly above the new-turned grave, and above the plain black coffin that held Sam Hughes.

During the brief ceremony, Rick caught the surreptitious glance of eyes upon him, saw heads hastily averted as his gaze crossed with theirs. These were ranchers, the neighbors of Keystone, and he wondered what thoughts were behind those unreadable faces as they stared at Rick and the worn, tired girl.

He wondered if there was any feeling of guilt, for the help they might have offered in this fight to save Keystone but which none of these people had as yet ventured to give.

When the first clods fell and the small crowd began dispersing, Rick delayed a moment over that other, forgotten grave in a corner of the weed-grown lot. He straightened the warped headboard, looked at it soberly a moment feeling the girl's clouded gaze upon him.

"Les Thompson," he said, heavily. "By now he would have been a man in the prime of life, with maybe a ranch of his own, a wife, even a kid or two. But fifteen years ago he followed the Texas trail north, beyond Boothill, and now all he might have been lies buried here with him— wiped out in the fraction of a second it took for Vince Kirby's finger to tighten on a trigger—"

Before he finished at Willow Crossing, he told himself, there were questions whose answers he would have. But all that must wait, for now—wait upon the immediate problems of Keystone's battle for survival.

Mary Jane had said nothing for several silent minutes. But now as they turned away from his brother's grave Rick felt her hand tighten on his arm, heard her quick warning: "Kirby—"

Lifting his head he caught sight of the marshal standing some distance away across the cemetery lot, watching them narrowly. The famous silver-mounted guns hung about the paunchy belly of the man, and the flabby features held a look of suspicion.

But he did not come toward Thompson, though the latter waited a moment to give him time for any move he might be contemplating. He didn't seem ready to challenge Rick Thompson or the gun the latter wore strapped to his waist; he seemed in no hurry to take up the matter of that run-in they had had a week ago, on the station platform.

Was the famous gun marshal a coward, then?

With a shrug, Thompson turned his back on the man and took Mary Jane to where the horses were waiting. But holding the stirrup for her, he twisted for another glance at Kirby and as he did his eye narrowed in quick interest.

Vince Kirby had moved over and was looking

at that forgotten grave, bending a little to read the name on the headboard that he had seen Thompson contemplating a moment before. Suddenly the marshal jerked erect, head swiveling sharply. Rick averted his glance. But across that quiet earth, where all the dead lay sleeping, he could almost feel the look of the other man boring into him as he stepped up into his own saddle, and followed Mary Jane along the trail toward town.

So Kirby had learned his secret! Now, at last, the marshal had a clue from the past that suddenly explained the puzzling sense of familiarity which evidently had been plaguing him, from the moment he first laid eyes on this Rick Thompson stranger. Well, now let him stew over it a little. The results might prove interesting. . . .

Meanwhile, Thompson and the girl had business to tend to in town.

When they reached the railroad tracks they turned down them, rode along the loading pens to a boxlike clapboard office, and dismounted there. They weren't inside very long. When they came out again Rick Thompson's face was grim, Mary Jane's white with anger.

"It's a lie!" she exclaimed tightly. "I know it is! There couldn't be more than one ranch shipping at an off season like this!"

"Maybe not," Rick said, heavily. "But remember, your uncle knew when we would be needing the pens."

"You mean he—?" The girl turned to stare hotly at the closed door of the shack, but Rick stopped her quickly with a hand on her arm.

"No point taking it out on the clerk," he said quietly. "He's got his orders from higher up, not to know for sure who it was booked the loading chutes—naturally, Pierce wouldn't want advertising for the dirty tricks he pulls to try to stop us." He added, "It's my own fault! I should have had brains enough to know he wouldn't pass up an obvious chance like this."

She shook her head, exasperated and close to tears. "But what are we going to do? All we've gone through, trying to make this delivery date. And now to have—" Her voice choked.

Rick Thompson wanted very much then to take her into his arms, right there in broad daylight beside the railroad tracks, and soothe her. She had carried up too long under strain and worry and fatigue—and in that moment she was very like a hurt and bewildered child. He knew suddenly, if he had never guessed it before, that something had come over him, these past days of knowing this girl. He had an idea it was love.

But he didn't do anything foolish. All he said was, "Maybe we better go have a confab with the bank. Just might be we can get somebody there to listen to reason."

He hardly thought, himself, that he was doing anything but whistle in the dark, to keep up what was left of their spirits. Mary Jane let him help her into saddle, let him lead the way while they left the tracks and the region of the loading pens behind, and went at a slow jog up Main Street.

As they passed the Lady Luck, two men were loitering against a roof support there and watched the man and the girl go by with open interest. They were part of Brag Nabor's crew; and memory of the humiliation that bunch had dealt out to him, the last time he had ridden in to town, sent Rick Thompson's pulse to racing with a hot urge to move across there—now that he was armed—and settle his score. But he couldn't—not now, with Mary Jane beside him. A settlement would have to wait until a time when it would bring no danger to the girl.

At the bank the two from Keystone were ushered into the President's office. He was a reedy, yellow-skinned man with his name—Arthur Rogers—painted on a wooden sign that graced his desk. While he talked to the Carlon girl and the grimfaced Rick Thompson, he toyed with this sign nervously with dry bony fingers; it seem to give him confidence.

"This is most unfortunate," Rogers told them hypocritically, waggling his yellow head. "If it were up to me to decide I should be only too glad to give you time. But too many interest payments have been defaulted on this note. And I am only an official of this bank, you understand. There are stockholders—"

"There is *a* stockholder, you mean, don't you?" Thompson prodded him sourly. "Friend Pierce is pushing the steam at you plenty, I imagine."

Arthur Rogers looked even more unhappy. "Please! I see no gain in any discussion of—"

"Maybe you'll remember, Ollie Pierce himself is the one who took this loan," Rick Thompson pointed out, ignoring the protest. "It was him that let the payments slide; now that Keystone has changed hands he's using that same damn note as a lever to pry the ranch out of our hands and into the vaults of the bank. Afterwards, being a member of the board—"

"No no no!" the little man exclaimed, waving both hands in front of him. "I will not listen to such talk. Mr. Pierce gave unstintingly of his time and care to the management of the Carlon ranch, during the time of this young lady's minority. Unfortunately, Keystone just is not a paying proposition. It is not Oliver Pierce's fault if, despite his wise administration—"

"Oh, brother!" exclaimed Rick Thompson with a grimace. "Let's get out of here!" he told Mary Jane, shoving to his feet without giving the banker a chance to finish his sentence. "A fellow that can believe nonsense like that, we're wasting our time listening to him!"

111

"But what are we going to do?" she exclaimed, as they emerged once more into the burning sunlight. "Is there anything we *can* do?"

He didn't answer for a moment. He jerked the reins of his bronc loose from the tie post in front of the brick bank building, stood slapping the ends sharply against one hard palm as he scowled thoughtfully across the wide street, toward the weathered front of the Lady Luck. One of Nabor's men had disappeared, but the other still kept his position, in a lazy leaning against a gallery support that didn't fool Thompson any. He knew the man was watching him.

"Where's the nearest good shipping point west of here?" he demanded suddenly, turning to Mary Jane.

"Iron Wheel Gap is not quite a hundred miles—" she offered, quickly, her eyes on his as though she would try to read whatever thought lay behind them.

Rick was thinking rapidly. The audacity of the plan that took shape in his mind then was so great that he knew he did not dare explain it to her but it was the only chance he saw, and even though it meant not taking the girl completely into his confidence he suddenly knew he was going to push it through.

"Come on!" he grunted. "We're going down to the telegraph office and send that buyer a wire that his beef will be waiting for him at

Iron Wheel Gap instead of Willow Crossing. . . ."

She was too stunned, apparently, to begin her arguments until after the telegram had been filed and they were riding northward again through the silent sunlight. "But there isn't time!" she protested. "Even a hundred miles will take us almost a week to drive, all the extra preparations we'll have to make."

"That's so," he agreed,

"And we're too short of help. Even with Red and Pecos, we can't handle seven hundred boogery brush-cattle on the trail."

He considered this. "Yes, you're probably right. So we'll have to do some trail branding, then, to avoid losing them entirely if they scatter."

"Branding!" she cried. "Why, half of those mavericks have run wild since they were weaned. Think how much work it will be to try and slap hot irons on three-four hundred head of full grown steers!"

"Can't be helped," he said with a shrug. "It's part of the job." And then he grinned a little. "Still, maybe we can make it. Want to lay any side bets, just for fun?"

"Oh, you—" In exasperation she struck one small brown fist against her saddlepommel, jerked her head away from him. "You talk about fun, in a spot like this. You make me so darn mad—!"

He began whistling, a thin little tuneless

melody. He didn't enjoy making her sore at him, but at least it gave her something else to think about.

It would be worse having her asking questions, maybe pry out of him the whole extent of the plan he was contemplating. She would have to know in time, of course; right now, he thought it would probably frighten her all too much. For the moment, let things ride as they were.

# CHAPTER XI

He did tell Nat Fenwick the full plan, however, as soon as they were back on Keystone. The old cook's face grew grim and solemn as he heard it through, and he tried to lodge a protest or two; but Rick Thompson answered all his arguments and left him convinced, though darkly pessimistic.

"I guess you're right," he muttered. "We're bitin' off a big wad of chaw, but don't seem much else for it. What about Janie—she know what you got up your sleeve?"

"No. Maybe I ought to have told her but I couldn't quite bring myself to."

The cook waggled his grizzled head. "What she ain't knowing ain't hurtin' her," he admitted. "Maybe she wouldn't let you go through with your crazy scheme. And personally, I reckon it's better to go down swinging."

"I hoped you'd see it that way too," said Rick Thompson. "That's why I dealt you in . . . Now, the first thing is for you to catch the westbound this evening, for Iron Wheel Gap. You know what you're supposed to do. And there's a couple of wires I want you to send from there." He pencilled briefly on a scrap of paper, folded it and tucked it into the pocket of the old man's shirt. "Wait for answers. You ought to be able to make it back, tomorrow."

"All right," the cook agreed. "I'll put on my store clothes and head for town." He hesitated, and lowered his voice a little, frowning. "You better keep an eye on that pair of saddlebums you hired. I don't trust 'em!"

"You don't?" Rick Thompson echoed in a tone of mild surprise. He hadn't told either Mary Jane or Nat about how he had come to pick up Red and Pecos—about the stolen cattle, or the bushwhack try they had had at him. Now he said only: "Why, I don't know why you should feel that way, Nat. But I'll bear it in mind . . ."

Kirby had been looking for Oliver Pierce, but it was late before he happened to run into the man hurrying up the sidewalk of Willow Crossing's main street. Pierce had a look of abstraction and he would have passed Vince Kirby up in the gray dusk if the marshal hadn't stopped him with an anxious word. The other stopped, swinging on him brusquely. "Well, what is it? I got things on my mind."

"You'll have more on it when you hear what I got to tell you," said the marshal sourly. His temper had worn thin, chasing after Pierce. "This Thompson—"

The effect on Pierce was magic. It jerked his head up, and put a harsh tightness in his voice as he snapped, "What have you got to tell me about Thompson?"

"Maybe we better move off the street first—"

The other looked about impatiently. "Nobody's listening to us."

"Okay, if you say so . . . Well, ever since that buckaroo hit town I've wondered what about him was so damned familiar. And today I learned, out at the graveyard." Briefly he told of seeing Thompson and the Carlon girl there, standing beside a forgotten grave. He told of easing over for a look at the name on the headstone—"Les Thompson," he added:

"It all clicked into place then. In fifteen years I'd forgotten—the name, and everything. Everything but the face!"

Oliver Pierce was staring coldly at the flabby features of the marshal. "I still don't know what you're talking about."

Kirby snapped his fingers impatiently. "The hell you don't! That express office job! Remember the cowpoke I salted that time? His name was Thompson, I remembered today after all these years. This Rick Thompson is a brother or something—he must be!"

The other man remembered now, all right. His gaze turned inward in reflection. He murmured slowly, "Well, I'll—be—damned!" And then there was silence as night thickened about the pair alone there on the wooden sidewalk.

"Do you suppose he's on to anything?" the marshal asked finally. His voice was hoarse. The question seemed to jar Oliver Pierce out of his thoughts; the big man made an impatient gesture.

"I doubt it," he grunted, "and even so, don't worry—he can be put out of the way. In fact, that's just what I was mulling over when you broke in on me just now. The guy is getting too big for his Justins.

"I happen to know he sent a wire out today, arranging for delivery of that seven hundred head shipment to the pens at Iron Wheel Gap; and that damn fool cook was in and bought a ticket for there on the evening train—to get clearance on the pens, of course. How do you like that?"

The marshal frowned. "Couldn't you sew him up there, the same as you did here at Willow Crossing?"

"Suppose I could," the other admitted. "But I'm not going to. I've been keeping Nabor and that crowd on the string, holding them in reserve; and this is where I play them. We'll let Keystone go ahead and drive to the Gap. There's only five of them, counting the girl, a stove-up cook, and those two damn saddlebums he was fool enough to hire. Brag Nabor can hit one blow and scatter that herd so far it'll never be put together again— not in time to help at the bank, anyway.

"Meanwhile every one of Nabor's men will have his orders to keep an eye and a gun ready for this Thompson character. With him out of the way, I doubt if even this 'Pool' that's backing him will try to stop me taking Keystone. And if what you tell me is right, then we've got a double reason for wanting to make sure of him."

"It's right enough!" the marshal answered quickly. "I'd even stake my guns on it!"

"Your guns!" Pierce gave the other a contemptuous glance that the dusk half concealed; but there was no covering the tone of his voice. The flabby shape of the marshal stiffened a little as he heard it. "Don't try to pull that old Wild Bill Hickok gunrep on me, you damned has-been. I know too much about you. I'll call your bluff!"

And he went on about his business, leaving the marshal to stare after him in dark but impotent anger—anger that was all the sharper because Vince Kirby knew the other had him pegged.

The next evening, when the train from the east made its brief stop at the depot, a strange threesome swung stiffly down from a Pullman vestibule. The last had barely put boots to cinders when the porter snatched his stool and darted back into the car. "Now, where the hell did *he* go?" one of the trio demanded sharply, in a voice that was cracked with years of wear. "I was gonna give the cuss a dime."

"I kinda think you hurt his feelings, Montana," one of the others said. "You shouldn't have

119

practiced your sixgun draw in the washroom while he was tryin' to sleep. It made him nervous."

"A man's gotta keep his hand in, ain't he? You wouldn't wanted me doin' it in the car, maybe scaring somebody?" He added, hotly; "How about you and that tobacco spittin', Andy? He didn't seem to care much for that nuther."

"Hell! I couldn't sleep. And they wa'nt no spittoons in them uppers."

The argument was interrupted by a sudden inhuman, ear-splitting screech. They both whirled toward their companion; this one, who had kept a decent silence until that very instant, had suddenly arched his back and was baying at the moon that swam high in the deepening sky. He shucked off an old stetson and sent it sailing overhead. With another whoop he dug out a sixgun from hip holster, but before he could empty that into the evening air the leathery hand of old Montana descended on his wrist, sharply.

"Quit it, you damn coot! You want to raise the dead? You want to disgrace the whole outfit?"

"I didn't mean nothin'," the other old man exclaimed, crestfallen. "Just felt like makin' a noise."

The one called Andy shook his head in disapproval. "Bill, you ever gonna grow up? We ain't no twenty-a-month cowhands, hittin' town for a celebration. We're ranchers now—property owners. We're respectable citizens of this town, and we gotta start right off behaving thataway."

"That's right," Montana chipped in. "So put a check rein on that noise and try to scare up a little dignity. Go pick up your hat and bresh it off. We'll see is our saddles and luggage stowed away in the baggage room all right; then we'll look to a way of gettin' out to the Keystone."

His burst of exuberance utterly quelled, Andy followed crestfallen as his partners headed along the cinder strip beside the depot. The train gave a lurch, banged couplings, with a hiss of steam built speed and slid on into the night.

At the baggage room, the oldsters managed to pester the attendant to wit's end before they were willing to leave, satisfied that their precious saddles and warbags were safe. Montana carried a carpetbag with him, containing certain valuables he would not entrust to the care of the railroad company. "Send the rest of the stuff out to our ranch tomorrow morning, my good man," he instructed the agent archly.

"The holy hell with you!" the man in green eyeshade and black alpaca sleeve protectors retorted. Then quickly he turned back on the trio, unbelief in his bugged eyes. "Did you say, Keystone?"

"Your ears are good enough, if your manners ain't," agreed Andy Isham, complacently. "Yep, we are the new owners."

"Half owners," Montana corrected him. "Come on—leave off this unseemly bickering. Tomorrow we'll send a couple of the help in with a buckboard to pick up our traps, seein's as this hoss thief ain't too anxious about buildin' good will, and a spirit of service to the community."

It had been stuffy on the Pullman. Now an evening breeze was flowing across the darkening earth and Willow Crossing was a charming pattern of lights and shadows as the three oldsters hitched along the quiet street, and a certain tension ran out of them as they caught the scent of sage and rangelands and knew they were home again, in country where they belonged.

"So this is Willer Crossing," Andy Isham observed, chewing thoughtfully on the frayed end of a handlebar mustache, his old eyes squinting about him. "I remember when that was a name to scare little chillern. Never come this way myself, in the old trail herd days. How about you, Montana?"

"Nope," said Jones. "We bypassed the place by twenty mile, that time we trailed a herd to the Bitter Roots—"

"Now, leave us forget the Bitter Roots!" Andy cut him off quickly. "For a couple of hours, anyway."

For the first time since his silencing at the depot, Bill Gornay ventured a remark. "Do you suppose that building across the street would be a good place to start asking for our ranch? My eyes ain't so good as they was—"

Montana followed the direction of his pointing finger. "Nothing wrong with your eyes!" he grunted, with heavy sarcasm. "You know damn well that's a saloon. Still," he told Andy, "don't reckon at that one little snort will hurt any. Wash the cinders down our gullets."

"Find out, too, how good the likker is here," amended Bill, pepping up considerably at the rare experience of having one of his suggestions accepted. "That's always an important item."

They trailed across and up the steps of the Lady Luck. It was practically empty. A couple of overhead lamps had been lighted against the fading day, and the woodenlegged bartender was ready behind the mahogany to take their order.

"Make it whiskey," Montana said, putting his carpetbag down carefully beside his cracked Justin boots. "One each—no more, anytime the kid here—" indicating Bill with a jerk of his thumb "—is with us. He cain't hold his likker. I tell you this," he went on conversationally, "because we're likely to be pretty steady customers of yours from now on. You see, we're the fellers done bought the Keystone—"

They caught the quick stab of interest in the glance the barkeep gave them, as he poured the whiskey into shot glasses, but they thought nothing about it. Nor did they notice when Hank

Brush, playing an idle hand of solitaire at a table in the rear of the room, dropped his cards and jerked his head to stare.

Brush watched a moment longer while they downed their drinks. Then suddenly he pushed back his chair and quietly slipped out of the saloon by a side door. He hurried along the darkening street until he reached an eatshack where Oliver Pierce, a bachelor, always took his evening meals. Pierce was there, in his accustomed booth, polishing off a steak and a platter of french fries. Brush hurried over and slid into the vacant place opposite his boss.

"Guess who just blew in!" he grunted.

Pierce, who didn't care for riddles, gave him a sour look and the other quickly hurried on to tell what he had seen at the Lady Luck. "Any one of the three looked like a good breeze would blow him over," he finished. "But so help me, they said 'Keystone'! They must be the 'Pool' Thompson sent that wire to the day he lit!"

The big man stared at his half empty plate, considering this. Suddenly he began to chuckle, solid laughter that shook his whole heavy frame. "Damned if this isn't positively funny!" he said. "Here I thought Thompson must have some syndicate or other in back of him—and it turns out nothing but three stove-up old cowprods!" He shot a hard glance at Brush then, sobering quickly. "Get rid of them!"

"Huh?"

"You heard me! There's lots of ways to handle Thompson, now, but this is one way that's worth a try and no risk involved. We convince those three old fools it's not a healthy kind of country, they'll pull out with their backing and leave Thompson high and dry—and Keystone ripe for the picking. Yes!" He slapped the fingers of one hand against the table edge. "Go back over there and get to work on them. We won't even give them a good chance to light!"

Hank Brush stood up, uncertainly, scowling. "I don't care so much for this, Pierce. Pickin' on old men—"

"I don't give a damn what you think about it!" Oliver Pierce snapped, though careful to keep his voice low enough that his sharp words did not carry beyond the booth. "You've got your orders. And if you have to kill one of those old mossbeaks, that won't break my heart, either. Now, go on!"

Brush nodded shortly. He was hitching up his gunbelt as he strode out of the eatshack.

# CHAPTER XII

At the Lady Luck, Bill Gornay leaned against the bar with grizzled old head cradled on his arms, and sang sadly in a mournful monotone. "Ain't it terrible?" Andy grunted to the barkeep, shaking his head in disgust. "One drink, and he's like that! I dunno when he'll grow up man enough to hold his likker!"

"He wouldn't of lasted two days, that drive I went with to the Bitter Roots," Montana Jones informed the woodenlegged one solemnly. "Why, the whole outfit lived on straight corn. The cook made coffee with it."

"Here we go!" Andy Isham groaned. "The Bitter Roots! That's why they call him 'Montana'—it's all he can talk about. Look, Jones! Ain't you got no shame, spending your life goin' around boring people?"

The woodenlegged man swabbed at the bar with a damp cloth. "You can't bore me," he grunted. "I'm a bartender. The stuff I listen to!"

"Oh, the hell with it!" muttered Montana, and stooped to get his carpetbag. "Let's hire a rig and get out to the ranch. I'm anxious for to see it."

"You won't see much of it this time of night," said Andy. "How do we get there, anyhow?"

The barkeep gave them instructions, and also

told them where the livery was. Andy Isham thanked him and took Bill Gornay by one bony elbow. "Come on, Bill. We're leavin'!"

But at once the old man started to wail and clutch the bar with both hands. "Naw! I do' wanna!"

Andy tried to reason with him. "We're goin' to the ranch—*our* ranch. We're—we're goin' *home!* Don't that mean nothing to you?"

The word broke Bill's hold on the bar, and he let Andy steer him toward the open doorway. "Home!" he echoed, tears dribbling down his leathery cheeks. "Mother!"

Andy shook his head at the astonished barkeep. "This ain't anything," he muttered sourly. "You oughta see him with *two* drinks!"

When they got out on the gallery, however, the night air seemed to help Bill some. At least it changed his mood, so that he suddenly began singing as Andy got him headed wobblily for the steps.

Hank Brush was coming up them just as the three started down. He quickly sized the thing up; his momentary attack of scruples had vanished under the goading of Oliver Pierce, and he had his plan of action all mapped out.

So it happened that old Bill Gornay accidentally wobbled against the stranger, and Brush gave out with an outraged yell. "Who you pushing, you damn drunk?"

"You had plenty chance to get out of his way," Andy Isham started to answer. But Brush was already moving in on Bill. He gave the old man a solid wallop against the side of the head, and Bill let out a squawk and went over backwards, clean off the steps.

Andy gave a roar at that and Brush turned on him, cursing. "You too, you damn banty!" He swung, a blow that should have piled the second oldtimer on top of his friend in the dust. But before it landed, something else happened.

It was Montana's carpetbag, swinging in a wide arc at the end of his gaunt old arm. The bag struck Hank Brush on the ear and it felt as though it was weighted with anvils. He staggered, tripped over one of his own spurs and went down in a sprawl on the steps. Then Andy and Montana both jumped him.

A wild confusion of yells broke out on the quiet night. The men struggling and writhing in combat there on the saloon steps made enough racket for a dozen brawlers.

Hank Brush felt suddenly that he was turned loose in a den of catamounts, against both of those old men. He managed to break away, but then he rolled off the steps and headlong into the dirt; and when he got to his feet again, Billy Gornay—magically sober all at once— was perched on the gunman's shoulders and lambasting him freely around the ears.

Brush's cursing rose to new heights as he reached back, trying to peel the little oldster from him; but Bill stuck like a leech. And now Andy Isham came in from the front, kicking his shins and sinking gnarled old fists wristdeep in the gunman's belly.

"Leave my friend alone!" he bellowed. "Put him down, do you hear me?"

"Damn it, I'm tryin' to!" screamed Hank Brush, almost sobbing. His words ended in a grunt as another wallop to the belly cost him what was left of his wind. He stumbled, went to one knee under the weight of the squirming figure on his shoulders.

Then Montana Jones pushed Andy out of the way and stepped in with an old hogleg revolver levelled. "Git off him, Bill. Stop kickin' him, Andy. And you, Mister, git on your stumps and out of our sight before we begin to act rough. Any skunk what'd pick on a helpless old man—"

"Helpless!" bawled the gunman. But he found himself free suddenly and he lurched up to his feet, cringing as he saw old Bill make a menacing move in his direction.

"Go on!" grunted Montana. "Beat it, now!"

The three little oldsters watched him stagger off into the darkness, blood smeared over his face and shirt, half doubled over the pain in his belly. From long habit, then, Montana blew imaginary smoke out of his gun and shoved it deep into a scarred holster. "Guess we learned *him!*" he grunted. "Maybe he'll leave peaceable strangers alone after this."

"Let's get out to the ranch," said Andy. "You know, I'm beginning to think I'll like this country pretty well. For a spell there I was thinking it might have got too tame and civilized. . . ."

Some outdoorman's sixth sense surely must have been what led the three, unerringly, in darkness and across miles of unfamiliar country to the Keystone spread. When they saw the lights ahead of them Montana let out a whoop: "There she is!" And Andy Isham stood up and cracked the whip, and the rickety livery stable buggy went rocketing down on the ranch with the three oldsters crowded together in the seat and clinging onto the framework while wind whipped at their clothing.

They made so much clatter and racket that the ranch came alive as they hit it. There were lights in bunkhouse and main building. Red Morse watched from the bunkhouse doorway, the gaunt form of Pecos silhouetted behind him. Rick Thompson, hurrying out from the main house, had an idea what was up even before he saw the buggy careening to a halt, the three figures tumbling out of it. The members of the Mossy-horn Pool caught sight of him and descended on him with whoops of greeting.

"Where have you mavericks been?" Thompson demanded, grinning.

Montana Jones stared. "Why, where you think we been? We lit out for here soon as we got your wire."

"You must have stopped on the way to have another look at the Bitter Roots!"

"Aw, naw!" protested Andy Isham. "We just took the cars, 'stead of hossbackin' it. Wanted to see Kansas City while we was at it, and that was a mite off the trail."

"Well, now you're here, step inside and meet your business partner and the rest of the crew. I'll have Pecos look after your rig."

Inside the house, introductions were brief enough but they seemed to hit the three oldtimers with a shock they would not soon throw off. Old Bill Gornay stared at Mary Jane for a moment of agonized silence before he blurted: "Great lovely dove! A female!"

From a corner of the living-room, where he had been looking on with a scowl of annoyance, Nat Fenwick demanded sharply: "Anything wrong with that?"

"I was raised on a bronc," the girl put in, defensively. "I can rope and ride and shoot and—"

"Don't mind Bill," Andy Isham said. "He's got as much tact as a snake-bit lobo. All's the matter with us, we're just plumb tooken by surprise, not

131

expecting to find our partner was goin' to be no lady—and a real purty one, to boot."

"Well, you better get used to the idea," said Nat Fenwick, sourly. " 'Cause this is the Carlon ranch and Janie Carlon still owns half interest—as much as the three of you mavericks combined."

Montana gave him a sharp look. "We know that, hombre. Don't need the help to remind us."

To Rick Thompson, it looked disturbingly like trouble growing here already. Obviously, Nat Fenwick resented these strangers walking in and laying claim to the ranch he had served so faithfully for so many years; while the three old punchers from Texas, whose life savings had gone into this Keystone spread, naturally felt a proprietary interest. He could understand both attitudes, but that didn't mean a serious rift couldn't grow out of the thing.

He changed the subject. "We better make a little war talk," he said. "And then we ought to get some sleep, because it's a heavy day tomorrow. By the way, you boys eaten yet?"

"Yeah," said Montana, "we cleaned up the vittles on that railroad diner just before we hit Willer Crossing." He was looking thoughtfully at Rick, noticing the way these past weeks had fined him down, hollowed his cheeks, gaunted his lean frame. "You don't look like you'd been puttin' on much tallow, boy. Something tells me owning our own ranch may have its grief as well as its gravy side. How about it, old hoss."

Rick Thompson nodded, tiredly. "We better all warm a chair; there's a lot to be augered over, and we might as well have it out now . . ."

They talked a long time, the discussion growing ever more serious as the night drew on. Thompson still held back, not ready yet to take anyone but Nat Fenwick into his full confidence concerning the seven hundred head shipment that was due. Nat had returned from Iron Wheel Gap that morning with satisfactory news of his mission there. Rick had received the answers he wanted to the wires that had been sent, and was grimly determined to go ahead with his program.

All he told the three Pool members, though, was: "First off, Keystone is trail branding, readying for a drive to start next Thursday. You three are going to have your hands full, starting as of now."

"We're *what?*" cried Andy, almost leaping out of his chair. "Now wait a minute! We didn't buy no ranch so's we could work our tails off! Why, this here was to be an investment, to give us some peace and rest in our tired old age. And you meet us at the gate with a brandin' iron!"

"The resting will have to come later," Rick told him patiently. "I'm sorry, but that's how it is. You don't buy a ranch with the possibilities of this one, every day in the week—at least not for the kind of money you were able to pay. I got you a bargain, but—" He looked squarely at Montana, the spokesman for the Pool. "I'm afraid I bought you into a fight, while I was at it."

Montana's seamed face was a cold mask. He said, curtly: "You better start talkin', boy. Just what are you trying to tell us?"

So Rick Thompson explained the situation, mincing no words; and there was growing anxiety in him as he saw the expressions of the three old men turn stony and unreadable. They heard him through without comment. He told of Pierce's ambitions to add his niece's fine ranch to his already considerable holdings, and of his attempt to hold Keystone cattle out of the Willow Crossing loading pens. He brought the story up to date, and ended with a shrug.

"I haven't any excuses," he told the three. "I know I've overstepped my authority, and risked your money on a bad deal. I thought it was worth the danger, but maybe you don't agree. And if you don't, I know that you're in a position to make it pretty tough for me. I'm sorry!"

There was a long moment of silence. Over in his corner, Nat Fenwick was fidgeting nervously, and out of the tail of his eye Rick could see Mary Jane Carlon with her hands knotted tensely together. He only wished the scene would get finished. He had bungled everything badly; now he had to face the payoff.

Montana shifted in his chair, exchanged a look

with Andy Isham. He said, slowly: "I admit this ain't quite what we was lookin' forward to. We had easy jobs on that Texas spread, and could of stayed on nigh forever. We throwed that over, thinkin' it would be nice to have our own iron and spend a peaceful old age sleepin' in real beds instead of on a bunkhouse straw tick. We wasn't figuring to use a brandin' iron or a gun no more, or ride trail herd. We're gettin' to the age where a hoss oughta be put out to pasture."

"I know," said Rick Thompson. "And instead I bought you into a slice of range war, and a ranch that's got both shoulders right against the wall."

"Speakin' of fights," Montana went on, and his question was a puzzling surprise to Rick. "Would you know anybody around these parts, kind of a stocky build, thick black mustache, carries one shoulder a little higher'n the other?"

"Why, from the description," said Rick, frowning a little, "I'd say that sounds like Hank Brush—right bower and handy man to Ollie Pierce. Have you met him?"

"Not formally we ain't," said Montana. "But where'd you think Bill picked up that bruise on his jaw?" His pinched old chest swelled as he drew a slow, deep breath, and turned to his partners.

"What do you say, Andy? This sidewinder Pierce never wasted no time extendin' his welcome, did he?"

Andy gave a sour grunt. "I knew all along that row was a put-up job. Well, it's nice to get your first licks in on the right side, even if you don't do it intentional."

"What are you fellows talking about?" Rick Thompson demanded. "Did you have some trouble with Brush?"

But Montana Jones, pushing to his rickety legs, waved his question aside. "We done talked enough for one night," he growled. "It can wait. How you expect a bunch of old mossyhorns to put in a good day's brandin' if we ain't had our sleep first?"

And thus the rift was closed. Swelled by three, the strange little Keystone crew formed ranks again, solidly, against the enemy. . . .

# CHAPTER XIII

Next day, branding was resumed.

It was a killing job; these were no yearling calves, but full-grown, two- and three-year-old stuff that had been allowed to run wild in the breaks under the lax management of Pierce and the Nabor crowd. Thompson figured that Pierce must have been intending that, sooner or later, these steers would wear one of his own registered brands; and until the time was safe to take them and throw them with his herd he had purposely seen to it proper branding in the Keystone iron was neglected.

Now the job was being done, out at the improvised corrals below the rim. Andy and Bill and Montana had worked as a team so often that they made fast time, despite their collective age and the wildness of the stock. With the Carlon girl helping Pecos and Red at another fire, and Rick himself pitching in wherever his services were most needed, the work that had gone slowly before picked up now and it should not take more than another long, hard day to complete the job.

The sun bore down. Sweat of men and horses mingled with the smell of the cow-chip fires, the stench of burning hair and hide. The bellowing of cattle sounded across the curses of the men as they wrestled the big steers down to slap the hot irons on.

At noon Nat Fenwick brought around a pot of coffee and some biscuits. Rick took his in saddle, swabbing dirt and sweat from his face with his sleeve. "Hot work," he said, grinning tiredly down at Nat.

The old cook shook his head. "Damned if I'd do it!" he muttered. "Knowin' that it's just a waste of time. You're gonna have some of these people sore at you, boy, when they come to find out what's really behind all this."

"Could be," Thompson admitted, handing down the empty tin cup. "But I don't think it can be helped."

He gigged his bronc toward the corral where Mary Jane and the pair of range tramps were working.

The Carlon girl, as expert as any cowpuncher, cut out the steers that needed working and roped them down by the tiny, cow-chip fire, where Red panted and strained to hold the animals and Pecos applied the branding iron. Both men had stripped to the waist; they were streaked with sweat and dirt, Red Morse's torso bulging with straining muscles, Pecos showing every rib through his skinny hide.

As Rick came in on the dusty, noisy scene now, a steer was bellowing under the burning iron with Red's knee on its head. Mary Jane had swung down for a moment to examine a shoe of her pony that seemed to be loose. She was on the ground, like that, kneeling with the hoof in her hands, when Red Morse stepped away and let the bawling steer lunge to its feet.

It swung away from the fire. Its staring eyes, wild with pain and fright, fell upon the girl and at once the lowered head snapped forward. Even before it lunged Rick Thompson, watching from a short distance, saw what was going to happen.

He gave a shout, a futile cry of warning. At the same instant he was slapping in spurs and putting his bay at a hard run toward the girl. Red and Pecos stood by the fire, without moving, watching this. Now the ironshod hoof of the bronc thudding in the earth mingled with the pound of the charging steer. Rick, racing in, gauged distances. It would be close, very close. . . .

Mary Jane had whirled, staring, petrified with horror and unable to move. The steer was only a fraction more than a yard away from her when Thompson's bay struck it sidelong, with one heavy muscled shoulder.

The steer was hurled off stride, stumbled. The bronc almost went down from the smashing impact but kept its feet, somehow. And then Rick Thompson was leaning from saddle, whipping one arm about the girl as he flashed by and swinging her up to him. Her pony had wheeled and bolted, squealing with fright. Thompson dragged his bay to a quick halt.

She was clinging to him, and his arm could feel the tremble of her body through the thin cloth of her shirt. When he moved to set her upon her feet again she seized his arm and for a moment would not let go. Leaning from saddle, his face just above her own, he said soothingly, "It's all right. You're all right now!"

He thought she was going to cry. Her lower lip trembled and her eyes brimmed with the shine of tears; but it was only the aftermath of fear. She let go of his arm and he straightened, dragged his bronc around. His face was set, his eyes rock hard.

Dust that had been stirred up was settling again, streaking the heated air with its tawny yellow. The steer that had caused the trouble was gone, on a dead run across the sage flats. And Red Morse and Pecos stood as though transfixed beside the tiny cow-chip fire, Pecos with the branding iron forgotten in his hand.

Rick Thompson kicked his bronc and rode straight in on the fire. He swung down, strode toward Red and without warning unleashed a hard right fist against the man's beardstubbled jaw. Red went down solidly. Standing over him, hands bunched into fists, Rick said harshly, "Get up!"

Slowly, the saddletramp obeyed, his eyes staring at Thompson, one hand covering his bruised jaw.

He was barely on his feet when Thompson jerked Red's hand out of the way and hit him again, in the same place. Morse went down a second time. And again, in that same harsh voice, that didn't sound like his own, Rick ordered: "Get up!"

But Red stayed where he was this time, sprawled in dirt and ashes, a slow flush mounting into his ruddy features and turning them redder than ever. His eyes held on Thompson's unwavering, and the cowman dropped a hand to rest on the butt of his holstered sixgun. "Get off this ranch," he gritted, "both of you. Before I kill you—one way or another!"

Skinny, black-browed Pecos blinked as the words hit him. He swiveled a look at the girl, then back again to Thompson. He blurted: "We didn't do nothin'. That steer got away before we were ready—"

"I might believe that," Rick said coldly, "if you hadn't once before tried to kill me, too. I let that slide—but this is too much. Now, get on your broncs and clear off this range while I'm willing to let you!"

The redhead pushed up to his feet, keeping clear of the sweep of Thompson's fist. There was blood on his face where Rick's knuckles had broken the skin. His expression was heavy but unreadable. He said, sullenly: "We got wages coming."

"Go and collect them from Ollie Pierce. You've been working for him all along—try and tell me you haven't! Now—fork saddles!"

They went without a word. They untied their ragged shirts from saddlehorns, shrugged into them and then swung up into the patched and battered hulls. Rick didn't take his eyes off them until the pair of range bums had ridden into the sage and were dwindling in size across the bottomlands.

He felt Mary Jane's touch upon his arm. "Do you really think—it was on purpose?"

Rick turned to face her, then. Her eyes were still large and dark from the shock of near disaster, the color only slowly returning to her face.

"They're a nogood pair of range bums," Rick told her. "They tried to kill me one day, on the rim; Ollie Pierce put them up to it. That's how I came to run across them, in the first place.

"We desperately needed hands and I was fool enough to think I could take a chance on them. Stupid idea to trust them, of course—to think they had any loyalty in them, or would really throw Pierce overboard. But I took that chance. And if they had succeeded today in—in getting you killed, I would never have been able to forgive myself—"

"Rick," she said.

It happened, then, with a suddenness that was not sudden at all. They must both have known it was coming, through the days leading up to that moment, and yet there was a breathlessness and wonder about it as she came into his arms, and they found each other's lips.

When they broke apart, finally, her cheeks were flushed, her eyes smiling at him. Rick felt the pounding of blood in his own ears. He tried to stammer something, but there wasn't anything worth putting into words. Her eyes and her kiss had said it all. . . .

The loss of Red and Pecos slowed the work down pitifully; by the following night, however, it was almost completed and Rick decided to call quits on the branding job. But on the tail of that came another split, and threat of trouble in the Keystone crew.

Rick Thompson and the girl were sitting around the office desk, quietly talking business but mostly enjoying the newfound happiness of being together and alone, when Nat Fenwick came uneasily into the room. His manner told that there was something troubling him, but he wouldn't come out with it for a long moment. He said it was a warm night, and went to take a squint out of the window, and monkeyed with the lampwick screw. "I'd better trim that, one of these times," he muttered. "Beginning to smoke . . ."

"What's the matter, Nat?" Mary Jane asked patiently. "I always know when you've got something on your mind, so come out with it!"

He whipped around on them, suddenly. "All right, I will!" he said tightly. "I'm quittin'! I'm handin' you my notice! Oh, not right away," he added hastily, at the distress that flooded her pretty eyes. "I wouldn't leave you in the lurch—heck no! But—soon's you can spare me a-tall, I'm pullin' out, quittin'—" he swallowed "—quittin' Keystone!"

"But you can't!" she exclaimed. "Why, you're part of this ranch—you've always been! You belong here!"

"Not any more, I don't!" He swallowed again, and his old eyes misted a little. "It's been sort of nice, since Brag Nabor and them was kicked out—just the three of us trying to keep things going here. But it's different now. Them up there—" he jerked a horny thumb toward the ceiling "—have spoiled it. I can't put up with things much longer."

"Montana, and the others?" she said, puzzled. "What have they done?"

"They just act like I was dirt!" he said, bitterly. "I ain't used to being ordered around the way they do—bein' called 'the help' and treated like I was less than nothin'. I put up with a lot from

Nabor's crowd on account of you, Janie, but I don't have to take it from them three roosters and I won't! I got my pride!"

Mary Jane cast Rick an appealing glance. Thompson was already on his feet. "Keep your shirt on, Nat," he said. "I'll see what I can do!"

The old cook had a grievance, all right. Rick had seen how things were going, and he figured it was time for a showdown.

Rick Thompson had been sleeping in the bunkhouse, along with Red and Pecos before those two were kicked off Keystone. The Mossyhorn Pool, however, had taken over an upstairs bedroom in the main house that once had belonged to Mary Jane's parents. They had scared up three beds somewhere, that filled the room almost to overflowing; their traps and personal belongings, fetched in from town by old Nat the day after their arrival, strewed what floor space remained.

Now as Rick entered the room it was blue with tobacco smoke despite an opened window. Stripped to pants and underwear, the three old men were lolling on their beds, tired from the long days of work. Andy had a magazine. Bill was trying to dig shred tobacco out of the stops of an ancient harmonica.

They looked up as Thompson entered. He closed the door, put his back to it. He came right to the subject.

"You boys ought to be ashamed of yourselves!"

"Now whata we done?" Montana demanded, quickly on the defensive.

"You know what you've done. The way you been acting toward old Nat Fenwick!"

"Well, how about the way he's been acting?" spoke up Andy. "Like he owned the damn ranch—him nothin' but a cowcamp cook, and a pretty poor one at that."

Rick said, crisply, "He's a good sight more than a cook! Maybe you didn't know it, but except for him you wouldn't have Keystone now."

The old men looked at him in new interest. "No?" said Andy. "We didn't know nothing like that."

"Then I better tell you some of the facts of life!" And in a few words, Rick Thompson related to them all that Nat Fenwick had done to hold Keystone together, and to aid Mary Jane Carlon when she stood alone against Oliver Pierce and the Nabor gang.

The three oldtimers listened with growing solemnity; Rick tried to lighten the mood by ending, "Last of all, boys, you want to remember cooks are scarce. A plain hired cowhand can cuss out the food and insult the potwrangler all he wants to, but you fellows are ranchers now. It's pretty serious when you get him so insulted he figures to quit."

Montana frowned. "Is Fenwick really quitting?"

"Well, I think I can talk him out of it for the time being, if you boys promise to go easy on him. Remember, he's got his pride as well as the next man. And you owe him a lot—we all do."

"All right," said Andy heavily. "We'll try to be good."

But then in a sudden burst of anger, the usually meek-mannered Bill Gornay threw down his battered mouth harp. It clattered on the floor, and the sharpness of his voice caused them all to stare at him in astonishment.

"Doggone it! Why'd I let anybody jaw me into buyin' a ranch for, anyway? You two smooth-talkin' jaspers! 'Be your own boss, Bill! Live on the fat of the land—a blasted king on your own half-wit domain!' Yeah—and what do we turn up with? Nothin' but the hardest work we ever seen, and no time for fun nor nothin'—when the day's over we cain't even relax by cussin' out the vittles. Me, I've had aboot enough!"

Andy said: "Hey! Where you goin', Bill?"

"That's my affair!" The old man swung his bowed shanks across the edge of the bed and was reaching for his trousers. They watched in silence, stunned by this outburst, as he climbed into his clothes, stabbing his feet into the old cracked boots, cinched up his belt with a hard jerk of horny fist. Grabbing his hat in one hand, and gun and belt in the other, Bill started for the door.

Rick said, "Bill—" But the oldster was already gone and they could hear his boots stomping down the stairs.

Andy Isham flung aside his magazine. "Plague take it! That young idiot's up to something!"

"Aw, let him alone, Andy," grumbled Montana. "You gotta remember Bill ain't much more'n a kid. You can't expect him to take things calm, same as mossyhorns like you and me."

"Well, mebbe not," muttered Andy, looking doubtful. "But I just hope he ain't up to some mischief—"

Rick Thompson got to his feet, a troubled frown on his bronzed features. "What I said about Nat Fenwick," he said. "You boys sure you understood how I meant it?"

"Oh, sure," said Montana. "We'll put a snaffle bit on our tongues after this. We don't aim to hurt nobody's feelings."

"Thanks," said Rick. "That's all I ask."

Going down the creaking stairs, he felt an oppressive weight upon his spirit—the aftermath of Bill Gornay's unexpected outburst. He knew that quiet Bill, usually the one of the trio that never opened his mouth or complained of anything, had said the things his partners were feeling but refrained from putting into words. And the weight of this was directly on Thompson's shoulders, for it was he who had drawn them all into this man-breaking proposition.

But when he went into the study and found Mary Jane waiting anxiously, the light of the lamp lying in a bright sheen across her hair and face, he managed up a smile for her. "It's all right," he said. "You can tell Nat I've fixed things with the boys."

She exclaimed: "Rick! What's the matter with Bill? He came tearing through the house and slammed out the door as though something was after him. And a minute ago I heard him ride out of the yard."

"It's nothing," Rick lied. "Maybe he wanted a little fresh air. . . . Now, what about those figures we were going over when all this came up?"

They settled down to the books; yet both their minds were filled with other matters and the numbers blurred in meaningless patterns before their eyes. It was perhaps an hour later that Andy Isham came into the room. Andy was fully dressed, down to his gunbelt and holster, and he said with a scowl: "I don't care what Montana says about it. I got a hunch Bill needs watchin' after. I'm gonna ride and find him before he runs into some kind of trouble—I know that crazy coot!"

"All right, Andy," said Rick. "Maybe it's a good idea. . . ."

# CHAPTER XIV

Andy Isham worked by the light of a lantern hung from a corral post, getting his rope on a fresh bronc and piling on saddle and gear. Tired muscles made him cuss some, as he dug his toe into oxbow stirrup and hoisted himself once more into the hull. "Damn that Bill!" he muttered. "Doin' this to me after the kind of day I just put in! Well, he'll be sorry by the time I get through with him!"

From long years of experience with Bill, he had a strong suspicion where he might expect to find his partner; he wasted no time now in debating the matter, but took the south trail and headed directly for town. It was a fine, large evening, with a high round moon swimming overhead and laying its silver wash of light across the broad and smiling land.

But Andy Isham had small attention for natural beauty, just then. He let his bronc out into a long, running walk and he held him at it—an easy, mile-eating pace for a cowpony. And as he caught the twinkle of lights ahead that told where Willow Crossing lay beside the murmuring creek, his grizzled head lifted and his jaw shot forward. He had a feeling things were going to happen before he rode out of this town again.

He reined his horse down to a walk, kept a careful eye on his surroundings as he came into the dust-deep main street. Things looked quiet enough—the usual night sounds, the gleam of lamplight laying bright squares across the warped sidewalk plankings, the dark bulk of empty, boarded-up buildings. But then Andy Isham saw something that knocked a grunt out of him, dragged the corners of his mouth down sourly. "Yeah," he muttered. "Bill's been here, all right!"

A carved wooden Indian, gracing the entrance to a cigar and tobacco store, had been neatly roped from its pedestal and dragged a couple hundred yards along the street, uprooting hitch-racks and scooping a furrow in the dirt. It had brought up finally against the end of a horse trough that was too solid to budge, and it rested there now at a forlorn angle with wooden hatchet upraised and a maguey rope still trailing from about its neck. With a sigh Andy reined over and unhooked the string, rode on rolling it up in his callused, leather-tough fingers.

"Just like Bill, leavin' a perfectly good reata. Plague take the youngun!"

Not much farther on he came to a mercantile store which boasted a great, glimmering window of plate glass. Looking at this, Andy nodded to himself. "Bill's still in town," he decided. "He'd never leave without first takin' care of that thing!"

Then he came in on the Lady Luck—a splash of light and piano music and raucous man-talk in the quiet evening—and saw a Keystone horse tied at the hitchpole in front, among the other droop-headed saddle broncs waiting there.

Putting his own bronc along side Bill's, he swung stiffly down. He fastened the rope he'd retrieved to the horn string of Bill's kak; and then, hitching up his pants and setting the gun and belt at a comfortable angle, Andy Isham spat into the dust and swung under the tie rack, moved across the walk and up the steps. Voices and whiskey-fumes hit him in the face; a look of contentment spread across his whiskered face, as he elbowed the swinging doors apart and eased into the crowded room.

For a week night, the place seemed to be doing pretty good business. Andy saw some games going; the wheel of fortune made a bright, colorful whirr. Over near the stage, with its dingy, dusty curtain, a piano player was getting what he could out of a disgracefully battered instrument, and a small crowd of cowhands were circulating around the bar. But, search as he might, he could find no sign of Bill Gornay; and this bothered him.

Wondering about it, Andy moved over toward the bar. Pegleg was working there, and Andy caught the man's eye, motioned with a finger. "Remember me?" he asked.

The aprons gave him a stony look. "Well?"

"I'm looking for my pardner," Andy told him. "The young feller that was in here with me the other night—one that couldn't hold his likker. You seen him this evening?"

The bartender said nothing. He favored Andy with an expression as wooden as his game leg, and then his eyes swiveled significantly to a point beyond Andy and at the same moment the oldster became aware of a presence at his elbow. He turned, quickly, and glanced up to see Hank Brush towering over him.

Andy's mustache lifted in a species of ferocious snarl. "You, huh?"

"Me," Oliver Pierce's right bower said shortly. "After what happened out there on the steps, last time, I just been looking for a chance to get my hands on one of you billygoats!"

"Too much for you, wasn't we?" snapped Andy. "I hearn the rest of that story. It was that buzzard, Pierce, sent you to mop us up, wasn't it? And you found things a mite more'n you'd figgered on— you was nussin' a nose bleed and one hell of a bellyache, last time I seen you!"

Years of gunwork had given Brush a permanent gunfighter's stance, with his right shoulder slung an inch lower than his left. Both shoulders lifted now, angrily, and a vein in the man's temple started pulsing. His mouth twisted under its roached mustache.

"I aim to take care of you three roosters," he gritted. "But one at a time—I don't like the way you gang up on a gent! You're the first candidate, grampa," he added. His voice tightened to a snarl: "So start grabbin' for your iron—any time you feel like it!"

Andy gave him a cool appraisal. "Don't git all bunched up like that, Mister," he grunted. "You ain't apt to live long thataway. And you're stark starin' loco if you think I'm gonna try matchin' my draw again' you. I know a professional when I see one; and me, I'm just a old stove-up cowprod, with rheumatism so bad it takes me all of a week to clear leather. You ought to be ashamed of yourself, tryin' to pick a fuss with a pore old relic like me."

"I'll wrastle that out with my conscience!" This oldtimer's talk had served to bring Hank Brush close to boiling. He stood there taut as a coiled spring, fury beating within him for release; his gunhand was lifted, splayed out, fingers an inch away from jutting gun-butt. "Damn you—*draw!*"

The sharp challenge carried like a whipcrack, and the raucous voices in the room sheered off abruptly. A circle of silence began at the bar, spread out, widened; heads were turning, eyes seeking out the danger spot. And then a shuffling of booted feet came as men cleared back quickly, out of the immediate vicinity of those two at the bar. On a discordant note, the piano died, the wheel of fortune stopped its spinning. Silence returned, blanket-thick. Only the banjo clock kept up its rhythmic sound.

Rage was a bright gleam in Hank Brush's glaring eyes. He almost screamed it this time: *"Draw!"*

The old man's Adam's apple lifted and fell as he struggled past a dry swallow. He shook his head a little, and his faded eyes looked away from Brush's livid face, glanced appealingly at the men that ringed them in, all hanging back and watching in silence. "Please, gents!" he begged, a quaver in his voice. "You wouldn't let him do this! It—it'd be murder, him against an old man like me!"

Some of them dropped their eyes guiltily, but nowhere in that watching circle was there one who would make any move to interfere in a shootout—not with Oliver Pierce's gunman calling the play. Old Andy's body seemed to droop, as he saw his death sentence reflected in those unyielding stares.

"So that's how it's to be," he said, in a dead voice. "Once, I might of stood a chance; but time bungs a gent up. I can't draw against you, Mister! Hell, I can't move no faster'n this—"

And to show them just how helpless he was, Andy reached down with painful slowness, bent warped old fingers around the handle of his gun and dragged it out of holster. The weapon was

155

battered by time, and looked much too big and heavy for the frail old man to hold it steady. But he leveled it, and his gnarled thumb caught the hammer and eared it back with a sharp click. And then he was snarling, in a startlingly altered tone:

"All right, you damn skunk! Get your hand away from that holster or I'll blow a hole through you so big they can drive a team and wagon through it—"

For a minute, as the crowd gaped, Hank Brush seemed hardly to realize what had happened. When it dawned on him how, under cover of that meek and pitiful talk, old Andy had actually drawn a gun right under his nose and had him cold across the sights, a gasp broke from the gunman and color swept high into his face. His right hand jerked, held itself just in time. "Why, you—"

"Easy!" Andy told him, face bleak, voice sharp and laden with authority. "I ought to gun you down, like you figured you was goin' to do a helpless old gent which didn't look noways dangerous. Well, it don't seem wuth wastin' gunpowder and lead. Here—gimme that!"

Reaching with his left hand, he snaked Hank Brush's sixgun out of leather.

"Now, git back!" he snarled at the crowd, a gun in each hand. "I don't trust none of you—"

They scrambled to obey. Andy Isham breathed a little easier, knowing he had them on the run—

and Hank Brush, unarmed and held at the point of his own captured weapon. He shifted a little so that he could see the bartender, and he said with a jerk of his head at a closed door across the room, near the dark and lifeless stage: "What's back there, Limpy? Behind that door?"

"Nothin'," grunted the woodenlegged one, sourly. "The old dressin' rooms—they ain't used no more."

"That so? Then how come I seen one of the aprons tote a bottle and a fistful of glasses back there, when I fust come in? How about it?"

Caught in his lie, the barkeep could only scowl. "I don't know nothin'."

"You don't know enough to tell the truth to the man behind the gun," Andy agreed, drily. "Well, I'm kind of curious for a look yonder. I know my pardner, Bill, is somewheres in the house and I sure don't see him out here."

Accordingly, he started for that door, crabwise, keeping an eye on the crowd and still carrying those two hoglegs. He heard the rise of voices, and through the rest Hank Brush's bellow: "Damn you, are you swipin' my gun?"

The piano—a battered upright, with its top missing—stood close to Andy, the pasty-faced musician staring at him scared-like. The old man said, "I tell you what, chum, I'll just lay it up here where you can get it."

But when he tried to balance the borrowed

weapon on the edge of the piano case, it slipped and dropped with a resounding thud and discordant jangling down among the works of the instrument. "Woops!" Andy exclaimed blandly, to Brush's bellow of rage. "Sorry! Maybe, though," he suggested blandly, "you're better off without it. Honest, I dunno how you've managed to live as long as you have. You ever get in another gunfight, try to draw your gun same time as the other feller, will you? That's the whole objeck of the thing—"

By now he had reached that mysterious closed door. He had his hand on the knob when a last, choked bellow came from the infuriated Hank Brush:

"All right, hombre! Go ahead—go right ahead. But you step through that door and I promise you'll be damn good and sorry—!"

# CHAPTER XV

For just an instant Andy hesitated, impressed by that warning. But the conviction that Bill Gornay was back there—in mortal danger, perhaps—settled the matter for him. The latch gave under his hand and he jerked the door open quickly, slipped through with his hogleg ready in case of need.

A shadowed hallway stretched before him, ending in a blank wall where a kerosene lamp in a hinged bracket burned faintly. Three doors opened at his left, a single door pierced the long expanse of blank wall opposite them. Everything was dusty and had a stale, airless odor.

Andy closed the door behind him and stood alone there, chewing at one end of his grizzled handlebar mustache. He could hear voices, near at hand; after a moment he judged they came from beyond the center door at his left and he prowled forward, cautiously. There was a big star painted on the closed panels, and a pencil-line of light showed under the bottom of the door.

And, unmistakably now, he heard Bill Gornay's sobbing voice. It was saying: "All right, Pierce, there's your deed. Damn your hide—take it!"

Without further hesitation, Andy Isham wrenched open the door, slammed it wide as he strode furiously into the tiny, smoke-blue room beyond.

It had once been the star dressing room, in days when the Lady Luck's stage was a regular stop for touring entertainers. The old makeup table still stood along one wall, and there was a dingily-curtained closet in the corner. A window stood open on the warm night, but with the door closed there was little air stirring.

Most of the crowded space was filled by a round card table under a hanging lamp, its top littered now with playing cards and poker chips and money. Bill Gornay sat with his elbows on the table, head in his hands, an empty whiskey glass at his elbow. There were three other players; Brag Nabor was one of them, although Andy didn't know him by sight. And he only recognized the stocky gent across from Bill by guesswork, and by the sight of a piece of paper in his hands.

"What you got there, Ollie Pierce!" Old Andy gritted.

They all were gaping at him, and at the gun in his hand. Andy's sudden entrance had taken them flat-footed and except for a quick, abortive movement of Nabor's thick fingers no one attempted a challenge. Brag changed his mind as the black muzzle of the old man's weapon swung around at him; he lifted both hands and laid them in plain sight on the table top, his face a glaring mask.

Oliver Pierce, himself, showed nothing beyond a faint surprise. "How did you get in here?" he snapped. "How'd you get past Hank?"

"It'd tooken more than him to keep me out," snapped Andy, "when I'm looking for my pardner!" But when he had a better look at the oldtimer and the empty glass, he made a sour grimace. "Another cryin' jag, huh? They plied you with likker and got you in this kind of a shape!" He glared across at Pierce. "I done asked you once, what's that paper you're holding?"

"It's a deed," Bill made answer, lifting his whiskered face. Tears were dribbling down through its leathery creases. "A quit-claim deed to Keystone. He won it off me, fair and square—"

"That's likely!" Andy snorted, derisively. "You're too young and trustin' to know! Lemme see them kyards!"

He snatched up part of the deck, held his gun steady while he fanned the pasteboards in his free hand, quickly scanning the backs and edges. A frown creased his brow. "Hmm. I admit they don't look like no readers or strippers—"

"Certainly not!" snapped Pierce. "It was a fair game, and a fair deal."

Poor Bill whimpered, "I thought sure I'd take that last pot. I was asettin' here with four queens."

"And what was this curly wolf holdin'?"

"Four aces!"

Oliver Pierce said, scornfully: "How about it?

161

Are you going to be so cheap as to use a gun and take back by force what was lost honestly?"

Andy's face colored. "No I ain't!" he snapped. "But damn it, what was lost honest can be won back the same way." He stabbed his gun suddenly into holster, slammed the cards down onto the center of the table. "Come on—somebody deal 'em. I'll sit in a hand and show you younkers some things about poker you never even seen before!"

At that moment Hank Brush came hurrying in. He had borrowed a gun from somebody and he threw down on Andy with it. "This old hellion tricked me, Ollie," he gritted, tightly. "But I'll take him out of here for you."

"It's all right, Hank," his boss said smoothly. He was already reaching for the scattered cards. "Let him alone."

"But he—"

"Let him alone, I said! We're playing cards!" Pierce jerked his head meaningly. "Beat it!"

Disgruntled, Hank Brush reluctantly pouched his gun. They heard his boots shuffle along the hall and the slam of the door leading into the noisy bar.

Andy had spotted an empty chair against the wall. He dragged it forward, dropped into it next to Bill. His partner turned to him with a tearful look. "Don't do it! Don't go risk your share of the ranch, too! After all," he added, "what Pierce won from me ain't enough to hurt the rest of you. What's a third of one half?"

"How the hell would I know?" growled Andy. "I quit school on account of fractions."

"It's a sixth," Oliver Pierce put in helpfully, as he began flashing out the cards, five around. "Not much in itself—but added to a half interest would give me control of Keystone."

"Whata you mean, half interest?" Andy challenged. And then: "Hey! Are you by any chance referrin' to Miss Carlon's share?"

Pierce shrugged blandly, put down the deck and gathered up his hand. "I'm her only living relative," he pointed out. "And naturally, if anything happened—"

"I don't like the way you said that!" The old man was on his feet, glaring darkly across the table. Pierce lifted his head, met his glance with eyes that were like chipped stone. For a moment there was silence, with Brag Nabor and the other man watching narrowly, and the kerosene lamp putting its yellow light downward upon the group around the table.

"Play your cards, Mister," Oliver Pierce said then, coldly. "You cut yourself into this deal— now, put up or shut up! Your share of Keystone against this deed." He tapped the paper with a blunt finger.

Slowly, Andy Isham let himself back into his chair. He was trembling with rage and on the verge of a heated answer when he saw Pierce's glance move suddenly past him, toward the open door.

"Howdy," said a new voice.

Two men slouched forward into the room. Andy went tense as he lifted his head and saw them—Red Morse and Pecos.

"Hank isn't doing a very good job out there," growled Pierce. "What do you two want?"

Red was looking over the layout, a grin on his stubble-bearded features. "Poker. . . . How about it, Pecos—shall we sit in?"

The gaunt Pecos nodded. Oliver Pierce rapped harshly: "This here is a private game!"

"And that's just the way I like 'em," replied Red, unperturbed. He moved around the table, slapped Brag Nabor familiarly on one thick shoulder. "How you doin', hombre?"

"Git your hand off me!" snarled Brag.

There was an empty box in the corner. Red hooked it with a boot toe, dragged it over. But as he sat down Andy Isham slammed the flat of a hand on the table top.

"I won't play with this pair of rats!" he shouted. "That's final! We fired 'em off the Keystone today. I don't reckon," he added, glaring at Pierce, "I have to tell you whut for . . . Rick Thompson ordered 'em out of the country—and I'll be damned if I have to play kyards with 'em."

Red gave him a frosty look, and Pierce's stare

was unreadable as he said: "I don't know what you're trying to insinuate, oldtimer, but I don't like your tone. Go ahead, boys—sit in the game, if you think you can stand the pace." He smirked. "Really, I dunno where a couple of tramps like you would get the cash for the kind of stakes we're playing." He picked up the deed Bill had signed, tossed it into the center of the table. "Here's the ante."

Reaching for the paper, Red Morse glanced over it and gave a low whistle. "Purty good! I wouldn't mind owning a piece of Keystone. I got a score to settle with that Thompson ranny, anyway, for kickin' me off the place." He nodded to Pierce. "Go ahead—deal the pasteboards."

"The ante?" repeated Pierce, heavily.

The saddletramp tapped the table top with one grimy finger. "You just deal 'em!" he retorted. "Because I got a hunch I'm gonna win this hand. And don't worry—if I lose, I'll pay off. Heard tell there's a twenty thousand dollar gold shipment in the express office safe tonight—and I trust you didn't have an eye on that for yourself—"

Andy Isham had a feeling of crosscurrents he wasn't able to grasp. He caught the meaningful look exchanged by Red and Oliver Pierce, and the anger coloring the latter's face; there was something hidden, here. But he gave the puzzle up with a shrug and reached for the hand Oliver Pierce had dealt him. No further use protesting the saddletramp pair being in the game—they were both already seated and had been dealt cards.

"I can't open," growled Red, at Pierce's left. "Who's got Jacks or better?"

As it turned out, nobody had. There were mutterings of disgust as they pitched in their worthless hands and the deal went to Red Morse.

Old Andy was beginning to feel the tension of this scene, as he stared at the deed Bill had signed, lying in the center of the table, and realized just what he had committed himself to. If he lost this hand, his own quit-claim deed would go into the hands of one of these tough gents around the table. . . . Bill was already out of the playing, sitting back now with a look of misery on his whiskered face. The others had met the high ante, and the cards were coming around again under the shoveling of Red's grimy thumb. Andy waited until all were out and then shakily picked up his own hand, card by card.

Four clubs, and the ace of spades; a useless, busted flush!

Gone cold inside, he cursed himself. Why hadn't he used common sense and kept the advantage a drawn gun had given him? Why let honesty hold his hand, dealing with this bunch of crooks? He should have collected that deed, at gun's point, and taken Bill out of here the same way. But too late for that, now. If he tried a draw they would easily blast him down.

"I'll open," grunted Brag Nabor. He shoved a wad of bills into the center of the table. With a groan, Andy shook his head.

"There's a bronc and saddle at the hitchrack out front," he said. "They're in the pot."

Pecos threw in his cards, but the rest of them stayed. Pierce looked sharply at Red. "Where's your money?"

"I told you—in that strong box at the express office," said Red, grinning audaciously. "Why, don't you think I can deliver? Come on, come on—stop worrying about it! Who wants cards?"

Because he really had nothing to draw to, Andy Isham took a wild chance and discarded the ace of spades. Red said, "Hmm. There's a man with two pairs," and shoveled out a card. Andy looked at it, lying out there on the table. He gulped, drummed his fingers, afraid to learn the worst. And then, frantically, he reached out and scooped it up, stuck it into his hand and with a silent prayer, fanned them out.

He still held five black cards—all of them clubs!

It took an effort to keep from sliding out of his chair, as that hit him. At Andy's right, Brag Nabor was saying: "The pot's big enough for me. I'll check the bets."

"Me—me too," gulped Andy.

"I'll raise," grunted Pierce, tossing in a couple of double eagles.

Red Morse rapped the table with his knuckles. "I'll let it ride. . . . The strong box," he murmured, at Pierce's sharp look.

Andy dragged in a deep breath as he saw Brag Nabor and the fifth man toss their cards away. "There's a brand new Winchester repeater in my saddle boot," he said. "I'll bet it." It was a lie, but seemed justified under the circumstances.

"You're called, Ollie," said Red Morse.

With a shrug, Pierce laid down three sevens. Andy looked at them and then his eyes swiveled to Red. He had one hand beat, on the table. One more chance—Then his heart sank plumb to the bottom!

"That beats my three deuces," Red was remarking pleasantly, laying his cards out one at a time. "But I also got a couple of aces here—"

Anguish blurred his eyes and Andy blinked against it. A full house! The cards in his own hand crimped between his fingers at thought of how close his little flush had come to winning. And then something caught at his breath!

Staring at those five cards Red had spread out on the table, such a surging of anger ran through Andy Isham that he lost all normal caution. All at once he was on his feet, kicking over his chair while his right hand pawed for holstered gun.

"You dirty skunk!" he gritted. "Where'd you get that ace of spades I done burned a minute ago?"

# CHAPTER XVI

Righteous anger had given his arm a speed that
startled Andy himself; and it caught the rest of
them flatfooted. In a cooler moment, thought of
his own audacity would have scared him; but just
then Andy Isham was beyond any thinking. Eyes
blazing, he tossed down his own hand and jabbed
a stubby finger at it. "My flush wins!" he snarled,
mustache bristling. "Anybody deny it? Anybody
say I don't take the pot?"

Oliver Pierce cursed him. Brag Nabor looked
as though he would like to make gunplay, but
the others—Red Morse included—only looked
on as the old man snatched up Bill Gornay's
deed, and the handful of greenbacks lying in the
center of the table. He disregarded the silver as
too much to worry about; he had a feeling the
smartest move right now would be one way from
there. "On your feet, Bill!" he gritted, out of the
side of his mouth. "*If* you can still work 'em. Get
goin'—I'll be right behind you!"

His partner was already started for the hall;
apparently, the liquor hadn't untracked Bill Gornay's coordinations. Andy, gun steady, waited
until Bill was beyond the door. Then, with a
sudden move, he lifted one boot against the edge
of the booted poker table and sent it spilling over
on top of those men, while his gun arced up and

blasted twice. At his second shot the hanging lamp exploded, swung crazily, raining glass and burning oil down on the suddenly yelling men below. And by that time Andy was already diving out of there, slamming the door behind him.

A gun roared, a bullet smashed through the panel. Andy ducked instinctively. He saw Bill headed for the barroom door at the end of the hall and he yelled at him: "Not that way, you blamed idjit!"

That single door facing him in the long blank wall was unlocked and he leaped and threw it open. Bill came scampering; Andy herded him through, took a nervous look over his shoulder. There were yells inside the room they had left, a thump as the table was kicked aside; boots slamming. And just as Andy dived through the door after his partner, he caught a glimpse of Hank Brush charging into the hall from the barroom, brought by the sudden racket.

Then another door slamming behind him shut that away, and he was in black darkness.

Up ahead he could hear Bill Gornay stumbling and cursing; but he couldn't see anything. He barked his shins on something solid, almost went sprawling. Fumbling at his hat brim he got a match and thumbed it to life. He held it overhead.

Almost at once a draft extinguished it, but not before Andy had seen enough to know they had stumbled into the grimy backstage area behind that dusty curtain. A forest of flats, scattered props, dangling fly-ropes showed in the brief flame—and, yonder, a double door that ought to lead to something better than this.

He dropped the dead match, pegged forward. Behind him the door to the hallway wrenched open. Men poured in—but also, a faint amount of light from that low-turned wall lamp down the corridor. Andy Isham pivoted about, slammed a shot back there and heard a yelp as the men split apart to escape it. After that he had a grip on Bill's arm and was fairly sprinting for the exit.

Bullets slapped the dusty wall. Then Andy hurled himself bodily against the double doors and by some miracle they weren't locked. The two oldtimers spilled through, just beating out a hail of lead.

They were in the alley that ran alongside the saloon. Bill, scared cold sober now, made a beeline for the street and the rack where their horses were tied, and Andy was right behind him. Fumbling fingers had trouble with the knots; the two had just plumped into saddle when Andy sighted Brush and Brag Nabor coming out of the alley, into the light spilled from a lamplit window. A shot lanced the darkness—but by then the two Keystone broncs had taken the steel and were lined out along the street, too fast for mere bullets to overtake them.

Just as Andy Isham felt that they had escaped

from what had been as tight a thing as he could ever remember walking into, a sudden shot from Bill's sixgun brought him jerking around. The splintering of plate glass mingled with the weapon's roar; old Bill had his chin tilted at the stars, a long and eerie war-whoop trailing from him. As the broncs galloped on with unbroken stride, Andy muttered sourly; "I mighta knowed he wouldn't fergit that windy!"

Minutes later, the last building had flashed back behind them and the moonbright flats stretched ahead. They went pounding up the northward trail for another couple miles before they dared ease their mad pace and finally pull tired and blowing broncs in to a halt. Looking back for a long, tense moment, Andy keened the wind. At last he decided that pursuit had not followed them out of Willow Crossing.

"Probably figure they don't want to tangle with a couple of billygoats like us," he grunted with satisfaction. "Not in the dark, leastwise—be pretty scary fer 'em!"

He squared around in saddle, then. "All right, you pesky idjit!" he grunted at Bill. "Get that crowbait to traveling. But crowd my stirrup because I got some things I want to say to you!"

Bill Gornay listened meekly while Andy told him in no uncertain terms just what he thought of his partner. It went on for a blistering ten minutes or so. "I'm gittin' almighty tired dragging you out of the messes you get into," Andy finally wound up, out of breath. "You near got us both killed tonight, trying to save your share of the ranch for you. You savvy that, don't you?"

Bill cleared his throat noisily. "I—suppose you're pretty near right, Andy," he admitted sadly. "Only one thing—"

"Well?"

"That deed—I don't reckon it'd done Pierce much good, even if he'd kept it."

Andy snorted. "And what makes you think that, you poor goof?"

"Well, you see, I—I signed your name to it! After that I was fixin' to just git up and walk out of that card game—except you come and busted in on us. . . ."

Andy Isham was silent.

It was close to midnight when they rode in on Keystone, and stripped their lathered horses and turned them into the starveout. They were spreading out the wrinkles in sweaty blankets when Rick Thompson came from the bunkhouse, barefooted, his pants pulled on hastily.

"Where you fellows been?" he demanded sharply. "I've been lying in there worrying about you!"

"A long story, Rick," said Andy, bleakly. "Just lucky we're gonna live to see it continued in next week's issue . . . Set down and we'll tell you about it!"

They perched on the bunkhouse steps and Rick Thompson smoked out a cigarette while he heard of the happenings in town. When Andy had finished there was a long silence, and then Rick dragged a deep breath and flicked the butt of his quirly away into the dust, its glowing end making a neat arc of cherry flames.

"So Ollie Pierce would be Miss Carlon's sole surviving relative!" he gritted tightly. "That was certainly a slip on his part! I don't put anything past the gent; from now on we've got to see that the girl is never alone and unguarded, at a time when she might be in danger!"

Andy Isham scowled in the darkness. "You— you think he'd dare—?"

"Now that he's tipped his hand, maybe not. Most likely it was just an idea that occurred to him when he thought he had gained control of a part of Keystone and saw where her half would give him the ruling interest. Since it didn't work out that way, he'll have to go back now to his original plans. And on that score, so happens I've worked out a little trap for him!"

"A trap?" echoed Bill. "What do you mean, Rick?"

Thompson stood up. "I'll let you in on that when it's time," he said. He added, grimly: "And that Red Morse hombre! There's coming a time, before this thing's over, when I'll settle with him! That's a promise!"

175

"Well now, Rick—" Andy's voice was suddenly thoughtful. "There's something funny about that bird and his pal, Pecos. I been thinking about it, all the way in from town. Something gave me a sneakin' hunch he was playing a deep game of his own in that room, this evening. He ain't as close to Ollie Pierce as you might think: looked to me like he was takin' digs at the guy—some kind of gag about the express office that I didn't noways get. But whatever it was, he had Ollie pretty hot under the collar!

"I'd go so far as to say he deliberately mishandled those kyards, just so's I'd blow off the way I did and come out holdin' that deed instead of Pierce. In fact, I think the guy's honest, Rick, and tryin' in his own way to help us!"

Thompson grunted his disbelief. "You must be outa your head, Andy! You better get you some sleep!"

"All right—have it your way. But that's what I think and I'm stickin' to it! Night, Rick!"

"Oh—one more thing," Thompson said just as they were about to split up—he to go into the bunkhouse, the other two to head for their room in the main building. "We held a powwow this evening, while you fellows were gone. Bill here is right—things can't go on as they have. We've decided we're going to push through to a showdown with Ollie Pierce—find out once and for all who rules this range!

"No more trail branding. By day after tomorrow the brands ought to be healed and we'll be ready to roll. We'll hit the trail for Iron Wheel Gap, with that delivery herd. And we'll see if Ollie Pierce has got what it takes to stop us. . . . That acceptable with you boys?"

Andy nodded shortly. "Suits me—"

"Dang it, yes!" cried Bill Gornay, with unexpected vehemence. "If there's a fight on our hands, get it over with—that's what I allus say. Lick this Pierce varmint, and after that we can settle down at long last and take it easy!"

"That's right," grunted Andy darkly, thinking of the bullets he had ducked that evening. "We'll take it easy, all right. Mebbe in Boothill!"

# CHAPTER XVII

It was slow, making a start. The separate holdings had to be thrown together—a tough job, because as soon as the pens were down the steers tried to scatter for the brush again.

The men cursed and drove their sweating horses in to intercept them, swung lariat loops and sombreros and shouted as they hazed the fleetfooted steers away from those breaks and out upon the sage flats. As soon as they had the beginning of a herd milling there, however, the other critters gravitated toward it from natural gregarious instincts. After that it wasn't so hard to handle them.

Noon heat was on the range, however, by the time they had the herd assembled. They ate in saddle, broncs circling the grazing animals, their riders already dusty and tired enough from the morning's battle. Dust hung in a tawny haze above the circle of red backs and horns. Rick Thompson considered the mood of the herd, and then edged his bronc alongside of Montana's.

"Let's start them drifting. We'll pick up Nat and the wagon and push on as far as we can by nightfall. Want to get these critters tired out so they'll bed down on new range." He added, "You've got plenty of ammunition, I hope?"

"Sure thing," said Montana, grinning tightly. He patted his shell belt, agleam with the shine of new cartridges, every loop filled. "Ready for anything."

Thompson reined about, took off his stetson and waved it slowly from side to side above his head. Answering signals came from the other riders. They moved in on the cattle then, and the drive had started.

Montana and Rick rode point; Andy and the girl came in at flank position, Bill Gornay brought up the drag. They let the critters drift at first, only pushing them a little and keeping them headed right as they went along, grazing while they moved. Gradually they stepped up the pace, and slowly the little herd began to take on characteristic trail-drive shape, strung out serpent-like in an undulating line across the rolling sage and bunchgrass flats.

At the ranch headquarters, Nat Fenwick had an old roundup chuck wagon loaded and ready. When he saw the dust of the drive he swung up to the seat and got his rig rolling, moving out ahead of the herd. Because Keystone was shorthanded, there was to be no remuda, each rider would have to make out with the one mount he forked. Nor could anyone be left behind to guard the ranch either.

They would head south, Rick Thompson said, keeping the red rim at their left until they hit a fording of Willow Creek just above the town. Swinging west there, they would cross the stream and then push on to Iron Wheel Gap, keeping in sight of the railroad all the way. "The tracks may help to cut a stampede if Brag Nabor's men start one," he explained; added grimly, "and in case somebody gets hurt, there'll be a chance of flagging down a train and getting him to a doctor!"

"I call that using your head," Montana agreed, nodding. There was not a one of them but knew to a certainty that they could count on interference from Pierce's tough crew, somewhere on the hundred mile stretch of empty flats between here and the shipping pens at the Gap.

Hours dragged out. Going was slowed by the efforts of the cattle to bolt from the herd, head back toward familiar range; the riders were kept busy watching them and swinging in to intercept these rushes and turn the steers back among their fellows. But gradually the rim dropped back, and Keystone graze itself. The treelined stream showed. Somewhere due south of them lay the forbidden town of Willow Crossing and, nearer, the fording they would use.

They came toward this in midafternoon. The steers, though still restless, were beginning to settle down and accept the routine of the drive. Now the ground sloped away before them, toward the trough of the stream, and far to southward showed a dim splotch which was the town. They were a mile from the crossing when Montana Jones suddenly pointed ahead, called to Rick: "Hey! What's that? Looks like the cook wagon—"

Quickly, Thompson spurred forward, and Montana joined him. "Could be a trap!" Jones growled. "Could be they've struck already. You suppose they've killed the ornery little cuss? Dammit, if they have—!"

Rick Thompson said nothing, but they both kicked new speed from their mounts and bore down upon the willow-lined creek. Yes, it was the Keystone wagon, tilted at a grotesque angle just where the bank dipped down to the fording. Thompson rode straight in, yelling Nat Fenwick's name.

Then as they hauled rein, the little cook straightened up from a kneeling position beside one of the front wheels of the rig. He had grease and mud in a smear across his aged forehead, and a sour look for the newcomers. "A busted wheel!" he grunted. "Smashed it going over a rock."

Montana started to swear. Rick swung down from saddle, took a long look at the broken timbers. The wheel was really splintered, the loaded wagon canted crazily over on top of it.

Jones, his anxiety forgotten, was yelling at the cook: "Of all the damn nitwit—Good gravy, couldn't you watch where you was drivin' this buggy?" But neither Nat nor Thompson paid any attention to him. Rick straightened slowly.

"That's going to be the devil to fix. Better take my bronc, Nat, and ride in to the hardware store and see can you get some strap iron. Montana, with this wagon blocking the ford we'll have to hold the herd on the near side until we're ready to roll again."

"Damn it, we'll be here all night or longer!" the oldster growled. "Thanks to the dumb, stupid ignorance of a lop-eared biscuit-burnin'—"

"Now, go easy on Nat, Montana," Rick told him quietly. "Remember what we agreed to? Besides, an accident like this can't be helped. Nothing to do but make the best of it."

But Montana's anger might have turned to mystification could he have caught the grin and the wink that Nat Fenwick gave Thompson, as the old cook turned to Rick's bay gelding and swung astride. Nat headed the bronc southward toward Willow Crossing, just visible across the sloping miles.

While Thompson went to work jacking up the wagon and taking off the broken wheel, Montana rode back grumbling to tell the rest of the crew about the accident and to help get the cattle halted. Thompson could imagine the reception this news got, with the rest of the crew. It made him grin a little, and yet a growing tension was mounting in him too.

The consummation of his plan was just ahead. And as it rushed upon him he could think of nothing but the weaknesses of his scheme, the long odds and dangerous chances it entailed.

The herd had been halted and was milling now, grazing on the stream's east bank. Hoofbeats drummed from behind Thompson and he looked up as Mary Jane Carlon rode toward him. The breeze of her pony's movement molded her shirt against her, tossed a lock of hair across her face. She had never looked more attractive, he thought.

She reined in, looked down at him unhappily. "Oh, Rick!" she exclaimed. "Is this a—a bad omen?"

"I'll let you know," he said cryptically, fashioned a quirly from Bull Durham and wheat paper, "as soon as Nat gets back—"

A half hour passed.

They let the stock water at the creek, then mill on the flat bottoms, grazing. At last Andy Isham spotted the bay coming at a fast canter from the south, and presently Nat rode up to the wagon. Andy and Montana and the girl were there, Bill Gornay out riding circle on the beef herd.

Rick Thompson eased to his feet, throwing aside a cigarette stub, and moved forward. He tried to keep the excitement out of his voice.

"Well, Nat?"

"Here's your strap iron," the old cook said, tossing down a heavy bundle. It clanked to the earth and lay there forgotten. "Everything's quiet in town. No sign of Brag Nabor."

Thompson asked: "The loading pens?"

"Plumb empty."

"All right." Drawing a deep breath, Rick turned to the others. "We're changing our course. We'll point this beef straight into Willow Crossing!"

For a moment they stared, while a breeze that rustled twinkling cottonwood leaves above the bright creek made the only sound. Then Montana gasped: "Whut did you say?"

Rick looked straight at Mary Jane. "I'm afraid I've played my cards pretty close to my chest," he said. "I figured it was safest, the fewer people knew what was planning. I hope you'll forgive me.

"I don't think there's a chance in the world that we could get this herd through to Iron Wheel Gap—at least, not without an awful risk of all our lives. Brag Nabor's crew is bound to be waiting somewhere along the trail, and they're too many for us. . . . But that puts them out of the way now, if we suddenly switch our plans and hit for the Willow Crossing loading pens, instead."

"But—" Mary Jane was staring at him, shaking her head in bewilderment. "You made all your arrangements at Iron Wheel Gap. I watched you send a wire to the buyer—"

"That was a blind. Ollie Pierce undoubtedly knows the contents of every telegram that's sent over the wire from that Willow Crossing depot; that's why I sent Nat to the Gap, the following day. He sent a second wire from there, informing the buyer to ignore the change of plans. And while he was at it he arranged with the railroad to have cattle cars here to ship our beef.

"All that's left to do is get our beef into the pens—and then hold off Ollie Pierce if he tries anything. I think it can be done, myself; we'll be taking him by surprise."

Montana gave a grunt. "You sure enough took *me!*" he muttered. "But I'm game for this if everybody else is."

"You don't hear me arguing, do you?" said Andy.

Rick looked at Mary Jane. She made a hopeless gesture. "I should be mad at you, Rick, but I guess I know why you kept all this to yourself—especially while Red and Pecos were around. I suppose the trail branding we did was just another part of the bluff to fool my uncle? Even the wagon breaking down, so as to hold the herd up until Nat could spy out the lay of the land in Willow Crossing—?"

Old Nat's eyes twinkled. "I told you she was a smart gal, Rick!" He shot a scowl at Montana. "I'll take up with you later them remarks of yours about my handlin' a wagon—after I'd gone and spent a half hour fixin' that wheel so it'd look like a sure-thing smash-up!"

Montana's seamed face colored. Rick said, briskly: "There's no more time for arguing. What we do now has got to be done fast . . ."

As though at a common impulse, the little crew went into action.

Rick Thompson swung astride the bay that Nat relinquished to him, while the old cook pawed quickly through the contents of the wagon and came out with saddle, blanket, gear which he hastened to slap onto one of the team, that had been hobbled and put out to graze. Andy and Montana went off toward the herd at a fast lope, to tell Bill Gornay the change in plans. Mary Jane started after them, but Rick spurred and caught up with her and she turned as he neared.

He reached, put one hand upon her arm. "Still mad?" he asked.

She looked at him levelly, and then she smiled a little so that her nose crinkled in the way that fascinated him. "No, not mad," she said, her voice tremulous, "just—scared."

It was all the assurance he needed.

Ten minutes later, under Rick Thompson's quick orders, they had that herd rolling again—this time straight across the slants toward Willow Crossing.

# CHAPTER XVIII

They hit the end of Main Street with a whoop and kept going, shoving the cattle hard, straight down through the throat of the silent thoroughfare. Doors banged, yells of alarm began sounding as this strange invasion hit Willow Crossing. Dust built up, the ground shook under the pound of cloven hoofs. The herd rolled through, headed for the stock pens at the foot of Main Street.

Rick Thompson, riding well forward, had sixgun ready and his glance raking the street ahead for sign of danger. At one crossing a man on a farm wagon held in his rearing, startled horses, cursing the tide of roan backs that flowed past him.

Then the front of the herd was abreast of the Lady Luck, just as Hank Brush exploded through the swinging doors and came down the broad steps, a gun in his hand and a look of amazement on his beak-nosed face.

Thompson fired at him across the bobbing backs, missed. Brush saw him then and threw down for a shot through the swirling dust streamers; but at that moment one of the steers at the edge of the drive was pushed up onto the wooden walk and Brush gave a yell and dived back out of the way, tripping on the saloon steps in his frenzy. In the scramble he lost his gun and it skittered across the splintered walk, out into the shuttle of legs and trampling hoofs. By that time Thompson had swept on with the herd, knowing Brush wouldn't be able to give any trouble without a gun.

It was a good many sleepy years since so much excitement had hit that one-time hellroaring strip. The thunder of the herd rattled the panes of blind and dusty windows, bounced back from the lifts of empty, false-fronted buildings. Sixguns firing in the air, yips of challenge hooting from aging throats, the four oldtimers of Keystone helped Rick and the girl ram their cattle through and down to the empty pens on the railroad switch.

And there, expertly, they got those seven hundred steers through the gates, into the confines of the stout timbered pens, that were weathered to a soft silver color by the years and scarred with spur marks, horn gouges, and the burning of a hundred different branding irons.

The little clerk from the clapboard office was out, running around and screaming at them, but they paid him no attention. Finally, when the last steer was prodded in and the last bars dropped on the big gates, he got to Rick Thompson and managed to make his voice heard above the bawl of the steers, the confusion of hoofs and clashing horns.

"Let's go inside and thresh this out," Rick

suggested quietly, dropping down from saddle.

A minute later he and Mary Jane faced the man across his plank desk. The clerk was trembling with anger and maybe with fear, too. "You can't *do* this!" he exclaimed, half choking. "Oliver Pierce has these pens booked. I told you that a week ago."

"He isn't using them, is he?" snapped Thompson. "Anytime he shows up with cattle to be shipped we'll move ours out. I happen to know it would take him twenty-four hours at least to get a herd rounded up, and by then the railroad will have cars here and our beef will be on them." He took the railroad company's telegram from his pocket, spread it on the desk. He continued. "We're not interfering at all with Pierce's use of the pens. Meanwhile, we'll pay the regular fee. You've got no kick coming."

They were still arguing when a step crunched outside the door and they turned just as Oliver Pierce himself entered, the paunchy figure of the town marshal shouldering behind him. Pierce's florid face was dark with angry color, and his voice boomed across the sound of the loaded pens, outside. "What's the meaning of this, Thompson?"

"What does it look like?" Rick countered. "We're shipping cattle—but from Willow Crossing, instead of Iron Wheel Gap where your tough crew is waiting for us. We aimed to pull you off the scent and I guess we managed."

Oliver Pierce was almost beyond coherent speech. He roared: "I'll see the judge. I'll get an injunction forcing you out of these pens!"

"Yes?" Rick retorted. "I'll just go along with you. I'll prove to the judge you never had any intention of using them—that you hadn't even made any arrangements for cattle cars. I'll prove this was all an attempt on your part to tie us up at Keystone. I don't think you'll be able to get any injunction issued, in the face of that!"

"Why, you—" The other started forward, a fist swinging, his holstered gun forgotten in the rage that held him in its grip.

Rick took the blow easily on a fending elbow, and then gave Pierce back one that came chopping solidly against the point of the jaw. The man was wide open for it. It pulled him around sharply; he hit the deal table and it went down under him with a scattering of papers and account books and spilled ink, while the clerk gave a squawk of horror.

At the same moment Vince Kirby, in the open doorway, made a dive for one of his silver-mounted guns. Rick heard Mary Jane's gasp, tried to get around and get his own weapon out in time to meet this danger.

He didn't have to; for the marshal's draw got hung up with his hand an inch away from gun-handle, and then Montana Jones eased into view behind him. Montana had his own hogleg rammed against the lawman's thick waist, and the oldster's voice rasped drily. "Let's sit this one out, shall we, Fatso?"

"Thanks, Montana," Rick grunted. He turned on Pierce, flat on his back in the litter of the floor.

"That's twice you've walked into my fist, hombre. Maybe next time we meet we'll have to really settle our differences." He jerked a thumb at the door. "Right now, I think you better blow!"

Pierce got to his feet. One leg of his trousers was soaked in spilled ink. He looked at it, and he looked at Thompson as though trying to find words that were expressive enough. But all he said was, "We may settle this quicker than you think!" And then he turned, jerked his head at the marshal who stood there under Montana's gun, with fear making a gray mask of his flabby features.

"Come on, Kirby!"

As they tramped out of the tiny office, Montana stared after them and then at the hogleg in his hand. A ludicrous expression spread across his face.

"Great, lovely dove!" he croaked. "That—that was *Vince Kirby*. And I called him 'Fatso'!" Gone suddenly weak, he leaned against the door frame.

Rick Thompson turned on the clerk. "I'm sorry about this mess—"

The little man wouldn't say anything. Rick and

Mary Jane helped him set the table to rights, pick up the strewn papers and straighten them. As soon as that was done the man grabbed a hat off a nail. "Closing time!" he said. He hurried them all outside, slapped a padlock on the door and walked off, briskly. Twenty feet away he started running.

"Well," Montana grunted as the three from Keystone moved slowly back toward the mill of cattle in the pens, "there's one jasper knows trouble's coming, and don't want no part of it."

Thompson, frowning, turned to the girl. "Haven't you any friends in town?" he demanded.

She saw his meaning. "None who has nerve enough to take me in—not after what happened to poor Sam Hughes. No," she added, firmly. "I'm sticking right here with you—I've got a .32 revolver in my saddle-pocket and I want to be here if a showdown comes."

"It's coming," Rick said grimly. "Pierce meant what he said!"

He cast a glance at the westering sun, that was already putting a tinge of ruddy sunset color upon the far sandstone rim, and twinkling in willows along the creek. "They'll probably wait for dark. Can't tell how many gunmen Pierce hopes to ring in; we know he's got Hank Brush, and the marshal, and probably some others. We're only lucky Brag Nabor is squatting out somewhere in the sage between here and Iron Wheel Gap, waiting for Keystone to drive through. . . ."

Andy and Bill joined them at the side of the high cattle chute, both carrying saddleguns. Nat Fenwick, they said, had sneaked over to an eatshack to try and round up coffee and grub for them. Tension was growing in them all as the sun dragged lower and shadows began creeping in out of the low places. Except for the stirring of the cattle, stillness lay upon this lower end of town. Nothing moved here near the switchyard.

Montana cleared his throat, nervously; as Rick and Mary Jane looked at him he started to say something and then hung back. Andy prodded him. "Go ahead, pardner. Tell 'em."

Rick Thompson frowned at the oldtimers. "You got something on your minds," he said. "What is it?"

"Well," said Montana, as spokesman for the three. "It's about Nat Fenwick—"

"Oh, Montana!" cried the girl. "Are you boys having trouble again?"

"It ain't that!" Jones corrected her hastily. "It's just—well, the Pool's been talkin' it over," he blurted, indicating himself and his two partners, "and we want to split our share of the ranch with him! Hell, Nat's been carryin' as big a load in this fight as anybody. And besides—"

"Besides," Bill Gornay chimed in, "they's no use havin' a cook you can't cuss out when you feel like it."

There was a silence. Then Rick said softly, "That's mighty generous of you boys!"

"It's—it's wonderful!" exclaimed the girl.

"But don't tell him yet!" grunted Andy, quickly. "Wait'll the fight's over and we're sure we still got a ranch! Fenwick's such a mean old cuss he'd likely claim we was tryin' to bribe him!"

"You tell him—any time and any way you like," said Mary Jane, smiling in the darkness. "And I love you for it, all of you! Personally, I say we're in this share and share alike. I don't consider half of the ranch as mine. It's just Keystone—standing together against the forces that are trying to destroy us . . ."

A large pile of ties stood nearby. Rick Thompson indicated them. "Let's stack some of these up in places along the pens, and at every corner. That'll give some kind of shelter to fight behind. When they hit, it's going to be from all directions at once!"

They fell to, hauling the thick ties, glad for something to keep them busy. Nat came with coffee pot and grub; but food didn't sit well on stomachs that were tight with apprehension. Five men and a girl, against whatever forces Oliver Pierce cared to throw against them . . .

A full white moon sliding up behind the rim, brought a night breeze with it, to breathe across the range and the town and tug at hat brims, shirts. As day faded out the glow of the moon strengthened, making vague the shadows of things.

The stock in the pens, fed and watered, began to settle down; a deceptive peace lay over everything, and a silence through which they could hear their own breathing and the gurgle of the creek around piles of the railroad trestle. Yellow lamplight shone in windows, up in the town itself, as the sky deepened behind the square cutout silhouettes of buildings.

Rick Thompson was talking quietly to the girl when a sudden outburst around at another side of the long line of pens brought him up and heading that way at a run. Angry voices sounded, a confusion of shuffling boots. Then as he came in Andy Isham was before him, saying tensely: "We corraled a couple of prowlers sneakin' up on us. Guess who they—hold still, damn it, or I'll blast a hole through you!"

Thompson made out the pair then, held under the menace of drawn guns in the hands of Montana and Nat Fenwick, and recognized them. "You?" he grunted. "What kind of trick are you up to?"

"No trick, damn it!" growled Red Morse. "We got something to tell you. Me and Pecos want to help."

"Likely!" said Nat, in heavy disbelief. "I got their guns, Rick. They ain't getting away with anything."

Red swore. "Since that accident at the branding fire, you've made up your minds we're no good, haven't you? You just won't give us a chance!"

Frowning at the redheaded saddletramp, Rick asked slowly: "What is it you wanted to tell me, Red?"

"Nothin'," the other answered sourly. "Only that Brag Nabor and his gang just hit town! That they'll be here in a minute to smoke you plumb out of here!"

"Nabor!" Andy Isham exclaimed. "But I—I thought we were shut of him. I thought he was coolin' his heels somewhere between here and Iron Wheel Gap—"

"He was," the saddletramp said. "Until this afternoon when Pierce heard your drive had been stalled up north with a smashed wagon wheel. I understand he sent a rider out then to call Nabor back in, figuring to make his try at you closer home. Anyway, me and Pecos seen the bunch ride in just now and we come to lend a hand—if you'd let us!"

Rick Thompson swore. That ruse with the broken wheel had boomeranged worse than he dreamed. No wonder Pierce had sounded sure of things. With Brag Nabor's crew back in town and mixing in this—

And then—here they came! Mounted shapes drumming out of the shadows with guns streaking sudden fire! Thompson whirled to meet the charge, the gun in his own hand rocking up as he hit trigger. Beside him Andy Isham was firing, too. And from the tail of his eye he saw Red Morse fall upon Nat Fenwick, jerk his captured gun from the old cook's waistband and twist about, drop to one knee as he too drilled lead at the onrush of mounted men.

He knew then, at least, that there was nothing wrong with Red and Pecos. All his suspicions of them had been false—saddletramps or not, these were a pair to ride the river with.

In the teeth of answering fire, the raiders had pulled back leaving one of their number crumpled lifeless on the open, moonbright ground. They were milling out there, reining their broncs, plugging gunfire at the defenders hunkered behind the inadequate shelter of piled ties.

"Spread out!" Rick shouted, his voice sounding thinly through the growing crescendo of guns. "Bunched up like this they got too good a target!" He himself moved quickly to the right, went into cover and emptied his gun from there. Gunfire made the night a hellish fury, with Pierce's men charging again and again, intent on wipeout.

All at once Rick thought of Mary Jane. Quickly he was up, running doubled over along the side of the pens. Lead slapped into wooden planks above his bent form. One bullet drilled his hat and lifted it off his head. Within the pens the herd was stirring, adding its frightened lowing to the bellow of the guns.

He rounded a corner into shadow, and he was calling the girl's name anxiously. Relief flooded him as he heard her answering voice.

She ran to him, clung to him. "Oh, Rick!"

"Keep down!" he ordered. "Hug the ground and any shelter you can find!"

But she wasn't listening. She cried: "Someone's in behind that shed, Rick. I—tried to drop his horse but couldn't get a shot over . . ."

Rick jerked about for a look. The little clapboard office was only ten yards from the pens and from its shelter their enemy was in a perfect flanking position. He had to be knocked out of there, somehow. Rick Thompson hesitated only an instant; then, grimly, his fist tightened on the gun and he was running across that open space, full into the moonlight.

A sixgun lashed at him from the corner, but its bullet whined narrowly overhead and he kept going, triggering reply. At his second shot he was close enough to hear the grunt of pain, the clatter of a falling sixgun as it hit and bounced off the clapboards.

Confident then that he had scored a hit, he lunged on recklessly—too recklessly! As he hit the shadows at the corner of the shack a blow struck him in the face, squarely. He staggered back and then he saw his opponent.

It was Brag Nabor; no missing that huge shape, topped with its hard little bullet of a head, as the man broke out of the shadows, came after him. He could see the shine of the ugly eyes. He glimpsed, in moonlight, a dark streak of blood across the knuckles of Nabor's right fist. Rick's bullet must only have grazed his hand, knocking the gun out of it.

The fist shot forward. Rick Thompson dodged it, swinging with the muzzle of his smoking gun, trying to connect against that hard, bony skull. He missed cleanly, was carried off balance. Then a kick from one of Nabor's heavy cowhides landed solidly against his hip and solar plexus. Rick went down heavily, struck on head and shoulders, slid a yard and stopped.

He lay there. The blow had knocked most of the wind out of him and paralyzed his muscles. He had lost his gun, didn't know where to lay hands on it. And now Brag Nabor was coming at him, full into the moonlight. He stooped for an instant, came on staggering a little under the weight of something that he carried in both hands, poised above his head.

It was a huge rock he had picked up, and he meant to hurl it upon his fallen enemy.

# CHAPTER XIX

Rick saw that coming. He knew it meant a crushed skull, a hideous kind of death; and yet seemed powerless to move, to do anything to save himself. He could only lie there and wait for it—

Suddenly, over near the pens a small-calibre gun cracked sharply. As its flame streaked the night Brag Nabor jerked to a halt in midstride. His knees buckled; he caught himself. Then he seemed to break in the middle and the weight of the heavy rock crushed him to earth, dead from the bullet Mary Jane Carlon had put into him.

That broke through the shock of pain that held Rick and he rolled over to hands and knees, found his gun in the dust and palmed it.

He looked across at the shadows where the girl was; he could imagine the tumult of emotions within her as she realized she had used her gun on a man and killed him. Rick wanted to go to her, but just then a couple of hardridden horses came pounding out of the confusion of firing before the pens, and instead he had to lunge up and dart into the shadow of the clapboard office, limping from the pain in his hip.

A couple of riders hauled rein, peered after Rick's scuttling figure, their mounts dancing nervously and pawing dust. "Brag?" one of them yelled hoarsely. "Brag! Where the hell—?"

"Brag's dead!" Rick Thompson shouted at them. "That's him on the ground in front of you—"

The crash of a gun answered him, and he felt a hot burn as of a poker jabbed into his bent shoulder. He triggered back. One of the saddles emptied, and as the bronc clattered away in terror leaving its rider on the ground, the other man gave a yell and whirled his horse, scrambling back out of range.

Thompson's foot touched something and he picked it up. It was the gun he had shot out of Brag Nabor's fingers, and it would come in handy. He checked the loads, was snapping the loading gate shut when he heard the sound of a tied horse behind him.

Turning he saw the bronc, maddened by gunfire, curvetting as it jerked the reins that anchored it to the hasp of the door. He recognized Nabor's gray, even as a sudden impulse sent him toward it.

With a few words Rick tried to soothe the beast as he got the reins loose, then vaulted into saddle. Spooked by gunfire, the gray tried to pitch him off. He got it straightened out, and then with his own gun in his hand and Nabor's sixshooter ready in hip holster, he drove that bronc straight at the tumult of gunfire in front of the pens.

A rider plunged at him. He shot and both man and mount went down in a thrashing tangle; Rick's horse had to swerve wildly to avoid piling on top of them. And now Rick Thompson switched the reins to his teeth and palmed his other sixgun. In the open moonlight, the attackers had been driven back by the snarling guns of the Keystone defenders. They were dismounted, firing from whatever cover they could find.

One raider was kneeling, holding his bronc's reins in his free hand. He whirled, swiveling his smoking weapon, as Thompson came at him; then after one hasty shot tried to scramble out of the way. Rick rode him down. He tried to leap the man's sprawled body but one of the gray's shod hoofs struck him in the leg and at the scream that went up from the ground Thompson knew, with a little sickness, that the man must have broken a leg.

Some of them had taken shelter behind an empty boxcar on a siding, were pouring in their lead from beneath its wheels and through the gap of the sliding doors. Filled with a recklessness that was beyond fear, Rick spurred toward it. He felt the gray stagger under him, knew a bullet had taken it. But then with a clang of steel on steel as an iron shoe struck sparks from one of the rails, he was across the track and swooping in on the half dozen men behind the car.

He came with reins in his teeth, both guns

smashing. The shots slapped thunderous echoes from the slatted side of the railroad car. The dismounted men scattered like quail before his charge, trying to target him on the lunging bronc but very few of their bullets coming even close.

But one man stood his ground, and the blast of his weapon seemed to sear Thompson's vision. He felt the tug of lead at his clothing; then he had the brightness blinked out of his eyes and dimly made out the form of the man, standing spreadlegged with gun levelling for another shot. It was Oliver Pierce!

He was sure of that, and it put a steadiness in his arm as he fired from saddle, triggering twice. Pierce crumpled. Then Thompson flashed away, leaving the boxcar behind him—and was suddenly aware of the alarming stagger of his wounded mount.

Before he could rein in, the gray went crashing under him. He leaped clear, rolling to his feet. A little dazed, he stood there in cinders waiting for the world to stop spinning. In that moment he sensed a difference in the tone of the fighting.

He heard a voice yelling: "Dammit! Pierce is down!"

"Brag, too!" another answered. "Hell, there's nothin' left in this—"

Rick heard a horse start away at a run, and then another. As Thompson went forward he saw Keystone men burst out of cover, coming with guns ready and yells of triumph. The firing had ribboned out, stopped. When he met the others, the raiders had gone except for those who remained as lifeless heaps on the moonbright earth.

Keystone hadn't come through unscathed. Old Montana Jones had a hastily contrived bandage around his head, on which his battered sombrero sat at a weird angle. Andy Isham's left arm rode limp in a bloody sleeve. But when Rick Thompson demanded: "Anyone worse hit?" they reassured him quickly, their old voices high-pitched with excitement.

"Where's Red and Pecos?"

Montana stared around in the moonlight. "Gosh, I dunno. They was on hand a second ago—"

Mary Jane Carlon came running, and he was quickly relieved to see her whole and untouched by the wild barrage of lead. She came to Rick and flung her arms about his neck, and she was crying. "Darling! You're all right?"

"Sure," he said, patting her shoulder. There was a bullet streak across his upper arm, but it had stopped bleeding and the burn of it was nothing he couldn't stand. He said softly, "Thanks to you, honey. I—"

She drew away. "I killed a man!" she exclaimed, the horror of it flooding into her voice. "I had to, Rick!"

"You killed Brag Nabor," he corrected her. "And he don't hardly count the same as a man. So forget it . . . Maybe you better see what can be done for that arm of Andy's. And boys, try to quiet those spooked cattle in the pens, will you? I got another chore to finish."

His tone caught their quick attention. "What do you mean?" the girl demanded.

"Vince Kirby," he said, grimly. "Tonight's as good a time as any to settle unfinished business!"

Nat Fenwick spoke up. "You'll have to hurry. I think it was Kirby I saw streaking south along the road out of town, while the fight was breaking up. I imagine he's quittin' these parts for good!"

Without a word, Rick Thompson left them.

He sprinted toward the rope corral where they had staked out their horses. He thought he would never get the bridle and saddle on, the girths cinched. With every moment wasted, Vince Kirby was drawing farther and farther away from him, and from the settlement of a fifteen-year-old score.

Then at last he was up and spurring across the switchyard. He glimpsed Mary Jane Carlon's slight figure, staring after him, looking forlorn and afraid as she saw him vanish into the night. He didn't let himself think about her—not now.

He hit the south road just where it widened out into the Willow Crossing main street, and turned into it. His bronc's heels drummed across the sounding board of the wagon bridge, were muffled again in thick dust. The town dropped away behind him.

But now, with the open trail ahead of him, Rick Thompson reined down a little, eased somewhat the first wild plunge. It could gain him nothing, only wear out the bay gelding. The road looped ahead, under the full shine of the moon, and it was empty. No sign of a horseman. And little chance of overtaking Vince Kirby now, if the man had that much of a lead.

But he kept on doggedly, not willing to give up. The night was still, around him, except for the creak of saddle leather, the thud of the bay's hoofs in road dust.

Looking up, Thompson saw in some surprise that a high haze of overcast had reached out across the sky. Did it mean rain? Even as he watched, the moon slipped behind this advancing sheet, its light smearing out into a broad circle of milkwhite radiance. At the same instant the glow upon the land dimmed considerably, the distinction between object and shadow blurred and made less sharp.

It was in this eerie half-light that he came upon the silent spread of Willow Crossing's cemetery, the graves and headboards sleeping under the sickly moon. And it was here that the gunshot broke with startling suddenness, flame lancing at him out of the tangled shadows to the righthand side of the road.

Almost without thinking Rick Thompson acted, dropping over his bronc's left shoulder and diving bodily into the ditch which lined that side of the roadway. The bay cantered off with reins and stirrups flying. Rick Thompson, hugging the shallow ditch, listened for sound of the ambusher across the road from him, but there was nothing. Only the silent graves stretching around them in every direction, and the faint rasp of night breeze in roadside weeds.

Vince Kirby was over there somewhere, lying low, probably thinking he had got his pursuer with one bullet but unable to feel sure. Rick had his own gun in his hand now. He had not reloaded since last firing and he did so now, moving cautiously as he reached to dig fresh shells out of his belt and shove them into the cylinder.

Then he threw the cylinder into place with a flip of his wrist and the metallic click sounded sharply loud in the night. And at once the gun across the way crashed thunderously.

Quickly Thompson snapped a shot across the roadbed, firing at the red-orange flash. He knew he missed, but his bullet must have been too close for comfort. For there was a slithering sound, and then the noise of groping footsteps. Kirby was retreating.

At once Rick Thompson came to hands and

knees, to his feet. The overcast was thickening, the darkness growing ever more opaque. Through it he went across the road, at a doubled crouch. He halted there with gravestones dimly white around him. Off ahead and to the left somewhere he knew Vince Kirby was moving slowly away between the rows. Rick started prowling forward, gun ready.

"The great Vince Kirby!" he called. "Running from a fight!"

"Damn you!" The curse came thickly through the darkness, and that other gun streaked fire. But it was hard to judge the direction of a voice and the shot was far from close.

Rick Thompson only grinned tightly, lips pulled back from the tense set of his jaws. He could have targeted that gunflash, but he didn't. He waited, and once more heard Kirby slipping away across the clipped grass of the graveyard. He followed, trying to avoid the soft mounds of earth that were invisible beneath his feet.

"I'm coming after you, Kirby!" he called. "Coming at you across the bodies of men you killed. And the grave of a youngster that was murdered to cover up a theft you committed under the shield of a town marshal's badge. You know by now that Les Thompson was my brother, of course—"

This time there was no shot. Instead, against the whisper of the night wind, Rick almost thought he could catch the strangled sob of the man's constricted breath. Kirby spoke, and there was terror in his voice: "It wasn't all my doing. Oliver Pierce planned that job. We split the express office loot two ways. He used his share to buy a start in the cattle business—"

It was news to Thompson—a stunning revelation.

He had never imagined until now that there was anything more personal between himself and Pierce than Rick's concern for the wellbeing of Keystone. He halted, digesting the thing Vince Kirby had told him—and in that moment of stillness the overcast thinned briefly, the moon's white face shone through strong and clearly.

Like the opening of a camera's shutter, the darkness fled and all the shapes of that eerie place took sharp relief—the mounds, the crooked headboards. Not a half dozen yards away the flabby figure of Vince Kirby sprang into sight as the light hit him. And the gunman took the first advantage of that light.

His gun roared. A hot stab of pain struck Thompson in one thigh and he went down, the leg crumpling under him. Kirby shot again, missing. Sick pain in him, Thompson lay sprawled where he had fallen, on his side across one of those grassy mounds, the sharp corner of a headboard digging into his back.

He propped himself against it, fighting back

the dizzy blackness, fighting to bring his arm up despite the weight of the heavy gun. Then the first shock of the bullet had passed and he got his black sights squarely on Vince Kirby's wide, moon-limned figure. When he fired he triggered properly, squeezing with his whole hand.

The weapon roared and bucked in his grasp. The figure of the marshal jerked with a convulsive shudder, spun half around. It fell.

After all the years, the legend of Vince Kirby had reached at last its ignominious conclusion. Like his many victims, he too had followed the trail beyond Boothill. . . .

# CHAPTER XX

Yet there was little exultation in Rick Thompson as he rode again toward town, with the first drops of the rain against his face. There was little of anything but tiredness, and the ache of his wounded leg.

The bay had not strayed far from the scene of shooting. It had been easy to catch; and Rick had found Vince Kirby's horse, too, where the marshal tied it when he paused in his wild flight to lay an ambush. The animal snorted and shied away at the smell of blood, but Rick had cursed it and crowded it into a corner and slung Kirby's body face down across the saddle, lashed it securely there with rope. Now, at a slow pace, he rode back to Willow Crossing with the led horse trailing, its reins anchored to the saddlehorn of his mount.

Aftermath from the ferocity of fighting had settled upon him heavily. His bullet-skewered thigh was bleeding again and he favored it as he rode; the doctor would have to take a look at that and quickly. But in Rick Thompson's tired thoughts a bullet wound was unimportant, compared to the tumult of emotions within him.

The score for Les had been settled, the blot

taken from his name. Too bad their folks weren't still alive to know . . . But the problem of Keystone still remained. Even though the fight with Oliver Pierce had been carried out to a winning, the survival of the ranch remained black with doubt. The sale of the seven hundred head of cattle in the loading pen would take care of interest payments due, but it would not touch the principal of that note at the bank.

With that note unpaid, a dangerous weapon remained in the hands of Rogers, the banker—and his was a power you could not combat with a naked sixgun. Thompson saw no reason to expect fair play from Arthur Rogers; it would be entirely like a man of his grasping nature to call that note in on a technicality and seize Keystone. And so, after all they had gone through, they were really no nearer to safety. . . .

Such thoughts as these were weighting him when he saw the two riders coming toward him through the misting rain. Even in that gloom he spotted the tall angular shape of one of the pair and he reined in sharply. "That you, Pecos?" he called. "And Red?"

They halted their broncs. "It's us, Thompson," Red grunted sourly. "We're pullin' out. We won't bother you no longer!"

Rick shook his head. "Why do you say that? You know I was a damn fool, the things I accused you of that day on Keystone. I wanted to apologize, but after the fight was over I couldn't find you."

The redhead shifted in saddle. "We—had some business to take care of," he muttered uneasily.

Pecos had sighted the led horse and its burden. "What's that you got?" he demanded. Rick told them.

"Kirby, huh?" said Red Morse. "Well, that's the last of the rats cleaned out. Soon as we leave, this range should begin to perk up and look respectable."

"Why are you leaving?" Thompson demanded. "You know there'll always be a bunk for you two at Keystone, after what you did tonight."

Neither of them answered for a moment. Then Red said, reluctantly, "Well—thanks. We'll keep it in mind, should we ever feel like driftin' back this way. But Pecos and me, we ain't much for takin' root. We like to travel. That right, Pecos?"

"Yeah," the gaunt saddlebum echoed. The battered hull with one cinch missing creaked under him as he shifted his long frame. "Fall comin' on, we thought we'd head south."

Red added, haltingly, "We—fell into a little cash this evening. Not much of a stake, but enough to keep us going. Oh, yes," he added, as though remembering, "here's somethin' else we found. Reckon it'll mean more to you than to us." He extended something, and Rick, taking it

213

in some puzzlement, discovered it was a piece of paper.

"Where'd you get this?" he demanded. "What is it?"

"It came out of Ollie Pierce's wallet—" Pecos began, but his pardner cut him off harshly.

"You have to tell everything you know? C'mon!" He already was spurring his bony cayuse forward, shouldering past Thompson and the lead horse bearing its still burden. As the two saddletramps went by Red called over his shoulder: "So long. Give our regards to the gal. . . ."

He sat for a long moment listening to the drum of their hoofbeats fading out. He thought, with a twinge of horrified revulsion, *The scavengers! Cleaning a dead man's pockets to get themselves a stake!*

And yet, amoral and without scruples though they were, that pair had done their part to save Keystone tonight. He could never forget that.

Then, digging out a match, he thumbed it to life and glanced at the paper in his hand. He gave a low whistle suddenly, let the matchflame gutter out.

It was the note against Keystone!

Oliver Pierce had paid the bank its face value and taken it over—just the day before, according to the dating of the paper. "He meant to foreclose, himself," Rick Thompson exclaimed into the darkness. "He didn't know he was going to die tonight—or that, without intending to, he was clearing Keystone of the last of its problems!"

The irony of this filled him with a kind of awe as he folded the cancelled note and shoved it into his pocket. And there was a sudden peace, as well, as he rode northward into Willow Crossing, and to the brown-eyed girl he knew would be waiting there, anxiously, to greet him with ready arms and lips.

**Center Point Large Print**
600 Brooks Road / PO Box 1
Thorndike, ME 04986-0001 USA

(207) 568-3717

US & Canada:
1 800 929-9108
www.centerpointlargeprint.com